LIVING GHOST

Copyright © 2023 Samantha Mina

All rights reserved.
ISBN: 978-0-9991577-6-3

Visit the author's website at www.SpectrumSeries.org
to order additional copies.

LIVING GHOST

Based on a True Story
By Samantha Mina

Other Novels by Samantha Mina

For the ladies and gentlemen
of the young adult community
at Reston Bible Church
whose love and prayers
helped keep
this ghost
alive.

PART I

"This next part, you won't believe."
"Probably not," I said.
"You won't. And you know why?"
"Why?"
He gave me a tired smile.
"Because it happened,
Because every word
is dead-on
true."

—From Tim O'Brien's *"How to*
Tell a True War Story"

BLANCA ROKITANSKY

Most girls grow up amongst a lot of pink. Pale pink bedspreads, sparkly pink sneakers, snappy pink hair-ties, dolls clad in garish pink garments. 'What's your favorite color?' the adults would ask. 'Pink!' the girls would usually cry.

Then, upon reaching a certain age, pink is inevitably replaced with 'cooler' colors—cooler in the adolescent sense, that is, colors that aren't so 'kiddish'—like blue. Most people choose blue, if they want to play it safe. By this point, the infamous question, 'what's your favorite color?' is rarely asked anymore. Instead, it's 'what color dress do you want?' or, 'what color would you like for your first car?' Hardly anyone could wrinkle their nose at the answer 'blue.' How could someone claim to hate the color of the sky that hangs over their heads every day?

The ones who fancy themselves 'rebellious' choose black. The ones who want to have 'flare' choose red. And, the ones who want to be 'original' often pick orange. Have you noticed how many colleges and universities have orange for a school color? It all started with Syracuse University wanting to be the first to claim a shade that hasn't already been made trite via hundreds of thousands of logo sweaters and jerseys. Soon, however, 21 other schools decided they wanted to be 'unique,' too. Boise State, Bowling Green, Buffalo State, Campbell, Clemson, Mercer, Oklahoma State, Oregon State, Pepperdine, Princeton, Rochester Institute of Technology, Sam Houston State, U Illinois, U Florida, U Miami, U Pacific, U Virginia, U Tennessee, U Texas, U Texas El Paso… even *Auburn* University is orange. Go figure.

I'd like to say that I grew up with just as much pink as the next girl. I'd like to say that I moved onto the blue phase when my age hit the double digits. Heck, I'd even take orange. But, I never got to pick my color.

Instead of floral pink wallpaper, I spent most of my time amongst white concrete. Instead of listening to pop princesses clad in fuchsia halter tops on an iPod, I listened to the *beep, beep, beep* of the ultrasound, tracing white lines on black screens. Instead of hanging with friends dressed in sparkly pink blouses, I holed up with bespectacled men and women in long white jackets. I've drunk more bottles of barium sulfate than cherry cola.

Even my skin is white, but not in the way you're probably imagining. Not white as in peach with a nice rosy tint, but white as in *white*. Like paper. Like hospital walls. Like lab coats. Like barium sulfate solution. My hair is white, too. Not the near-white-bleach-blonde-with-the-dark-brown-roots, like the cheerleaders at school. But, white like your grandma.

The only pink I get to see every day are my own irises. Except I can't grow out of those. No blue phase, there.

The world perceives me as colorless, but I always felt like I have a whole rainbow inside of me. I'm a part of the spectrum of humanity. The world just can't see it. Yet.

RUSSELL BROWN

It doesn't get any more obnoxious than that. I mean, really, there it is, in big embroidered letters beneath his name: 'BOWEL DISEASES.' Not even 'Dr. Benjamin Stuart, Department *of* Bowel Diseases,' or better yet, 'Department of *Gastroenterology*,' since that's a nicer way to say 'bowel diseases' without making patients want to puke upon first meeting. But, his coat just reads: 'Dr. Benjamin Stuart, BOWEL DISEASES.' I mean, *I* don't think it's gross; I'm not squeamish like that, or else I wouldn't be here voluntarily. I actually think it's hysterical. So much so that, every time I see it, I have to literally bite down on my tongue. Either that or laugh in his face and risk losing my job.

I'd like to say that I'm doing my residency here at Nation's Capital Teaching Hospital. But, I'm just a senior at District of Colombia High, so doctoring is still pretty far down the line. I'm just a volunteer orderly, after-school. Orderlies basically fill in wherever and wherever a hand is needed. Post-surgical NPO patient vomits on the floor after accidentally swallowing his throat-swab? I'll mop it. Receptionist calls in sick because she caught something from that jerk who didn't bother to cover his cough when he signed in? I'll be the one to take the front desk and talk with angry patients all day and schedule their torture-sessions until someone comes in and coughs on *me*. Patient needs a CT but the technician doesn't have enough barium sulfate to force-feed him, or contrast solution to stick in his blue veins? I'll go fetch it. Soiled sheets need to be stripped from the bed of a 77-year-old who just had a colectomy? Allow me. After all, it's not like a 17-year-old could really do anything to save a person's life for real.

It's only my second day, here—my first full shift since yesterday's 'interview.' I got to go inside an x-ray room on 'interview' day. On my way back from the ID office, a technician caught sight of me in the hall and asked if I could help him out for a moment.

He only held me for half an hour. But, those 30 minutes changed everything.

That's when I realized just how much I love the *swish, swish, click* of the CT-scanner as pale grey lights flash across the patient's gowned body. I love the weight of the radioactive shield on my chest, like football gear, but heavier. But, most of all, I love how the milky-white blotches and squiggles appear on the big screens after a scan. Whatever's making the patient sick, hidden in the recesses of his organs, now lights up for all the world to see, like a layered red target screaming, 'Hit me!'

That's when I decided which field of medicine I wanted to go into: diagnostic radiology.

When I first came to the hospital, looking for a department to volunteer, someone told me that help is always needed in Gastroenterology. No surprise there—there's certainly no shortage of upset guts in this age of super-sized fries and multi-pound burritos. Sure, the digestive tract is interesting and all, but there's no way I'm going to have 'BOWEL DISEASES' stitched under my name, one day. No, I'm going be the one to *diagnose* those diseases. I'll be the one who hunts down the bad guys—the one who gives a name to the suffering, so the rest of the medical staff can plan their attack. I want patients to say, 'Yeah, Dr. Brown diagnosed me, and now I have my life back. I owe it all to him.'

I remember when I first started developing an interest in medicine. My fascination grew progressively throughout my mom's tumultuous battle against Crohn's disease. Not that I haven't been hospitalized a fair number of times myself. I'm a healthy guy—an athlete, actually. An athlete with a knack for getting hurt.

The first of my major injuries occurred when I was 12. It was a Saturday evening and I was exhausted from hours upon hours on the Colorado slopes… but, I thought I'd hit the snowboard jump anyway—on my skis. Yeah, not the brightest idea. I don't really know what happened, but I think I sort of landed on my face and chest and went sliding down the hill. I wound up breaking some of the metacarpals in my right hand and straining my left shoulder. My hand swelled up like a fluffy pillow.

My second ski accident happened less than a year later, in Washington state. It involved a torn calf muscle and a face plant in rough, icy snow. My calf became a lumpy bag of puss and my cheeks looked like a hyperactive kitten went to town on my face.

The winter after that, I went skiing in Canada with a few friends from the junior varsity basketball team. I accidentally did a belly-flop off a 7-foot cliff and almost got ski-poled in the eye upon landing (thank heavens for goggles).

Hmm, I wonder why I still like skiing?

Anyway, regular visits to the ER throughout my adolescent and teen years helped open my eyes to a whole new world—the medical world. I became fascinated by the way in which the doctors, nurses, surgeons and orderlies would cooperate (or *not* cooperate) to make me well again. And, I decided that, one day, I wanted to be the star of the show.

* * *

"Are you Russell? Hi! Here's your schedule," were the first words I heard when I entered the lobby at 4PM yesterday for my 'interview'—

the first Monday of January 2009. I was expecting a handshake and a series of grueling questions about every extracurricular activity I ever sneezed at since leaving the kindergarten playground. But, a schedule? Did I have amnesia overnight, or did I somehow manage to get hired since coordinating this meeting the previous afternoon?

I stuck out my hand, hoping to revive some semblance of protocol. "Nice to meet you, Miss Ceco."

She took my hand briefly, then got right back down to business: "We're going to need you to take this form to the ID office, so you can get your picture taken and badge printed." She handed me a pre-filled contract. "You *can* start tomorrow, right?"

"Um… sure." I smiled, concealing my surprise.

And, just like that, I became an orderly.

* * *

I arrive Tuesday afternoon for my very first shift at the Nation's Capital Department of Bowel Diseases to the sight of an empty supervisor's desk and a sweaty young orderly wearing oversized scrubs, sitting up front.

"It's my second day," he greets me.

I chortle, "That puts you one ahead of me." I glance back into the office. "Where's Mary Ceco?" I want to ask her if I can be assigned to Radiology, right away.

"She's not here today."

"Do we have, like, a second supervisor or something? Anyone else I could talk to for some... direction?"

"Joel Ilea's not here yet, either."

I chuckled, "Mary Ceco and Joel Ilea? Man, you've got to be kidding me."

He blinks. "What?"

"Those names are hilarious."

Blink the second.

I gesture. "Come on: ceco, cecum; ilea, ileum..."

He continues to stare.

"Cecum, you know," my throat clears, "the first part of the large intestines, after the appendix? And, the ileum's the last portion of the small?"

Yawning, he stands. "Right, sure." Does this guy have *any* medical ambitions, at all? "My shift's over now, so here you go."

"Wait a sec, I haven't even introduced myself." I hold out my hand. "Russell Brown."

"Colin Jones."

Colin? This is getting too good. Laughter seeps from my lips.

His red brows scrunch together like a bushy caterpillar. "You're a weird dude, Russ."

"Is that so, Colon?"

"It's Col*in*." He pulls on a big brown coat, whose segmented puffs are just too perfect, all things considered. "Desk's all yours."

He gestures at the phone whose panel is checkered with an amazing array of lights and buttons, the computer whose screen displays an elaborate spreadsheet packed with names and dates, and an immense pile of unsorted mail.

The chuckles instantly die in my throat.

"Answer the phone," he says, zipping his jacket, "take down the caller's name, hit the desired person's button, ask if they'd like to talk to that caller. If so, hit 'transfer' again, then hang up. If not, hang up, hit 'line,' then 'transfer,' then the person's button, then 'go to cover,' then 'transfer,' then hang up."

Wait, what?

"As for the mail," he goes on, mercilessly, "you'll need to open each letter and skim through it so you can give it to the appropriate doctor's secretary, based on specialty, using the table posted here." He points to a strip of paper taped to the bottom of the monitor. "Do the same with faxes—they come in, like, all the time." He swings his backpack over his shoulder. "See ya."

And, with that, he disappears.

Apart from his rapid-fire half-minute spiel, I wind up receiving no other training on my first workday beyond tight-lipped, put-out, pained, one-word answers to the questions I ask of random employee passerby. I take patient calls, greet sick children and their grumbly guardians, and scout the office for the appropriate mailboxes in which to deposit scores of mail and faxes— all without a single clue. Are some of the calls misdirected? Of course. A couple letters misplaced? No doubt.

"Why did I receive this letter?" I overhear one doc complain. "Apparently, *some*one here thinks *I'm* Joel."

"*Someone* thought I was Bethany, earlier today."

I brush a wiry curl from my eye. It's okay. I can handle this. Just a couple more years and I'll be a technician. And, in a few more years after that, a radiologist.

RUSSELL BROWN

At 4:05PM, the large wooden doors open to reveal a short, eager-looking blonde boy in perfectly-pressed blue scrubs. Orderly the third.

He goes to see our supervisor, who gives him a brief greeting before promptly returning him to the front desk.

So, I share a shift this afternoon. Nice. That means 2-minute bathroom breaks won't result in missing 15 important phone-calls and 20 time-sensitive faxes.

"Russell Brown," I say, offering him my hand. "Senior at District of Colombia High."

"Jim Powell, freshman at Nation's Capital U," he replies.

Damn, his name is normal. Too bad. "So far, we've got a Mrs. Jejuno, a Mr. Ilea, and a Colin." I pause, hoping he'll catch on.

His green eyes light up. "For real? In a *gastroenterology* department?"

"Department of Bowel Diseases, you mean."

He tosses back his chin-length hair and laughs, "Oh, man!"

"So, you can see why I was hoping your name would be something more along the lines of... I dunno... Jim Jejunum."

"Right back atchya, Russell Rectum."

I fold my arms, amused. I decide I like Jim. "How about you take the phone and I take the fax machine for the first hour or so, then we switch off?" I suggest.

He stares at the vast button-covered panel as if it were bright white ambulance headlights. In the instant, it dawns on me: this is his first day. And, Ilea isn't going to train him. Sheesh, looks like our supervisor is taking a lazy-bowel approach...

RUSSELL BROWN

"Dr. Stuart yelled at me today," comes my greeting at the door. It's Joel Ilea. Guess I won't get the chance to go to Radiology today, either. I've been glued to Reception since day one.

He hands me a newsletter about gastro-intestinal surgery for small bowel obstructions, which I sorted the previous afternoon. "You put *this* in his box."

"The chart says Dr. Stuart gets everything related to the small bowels—"

"But *Dr. Patrick* is the *Chief* GI *Surgeon*. Dr. Stuart gets everything about the small bowels except small bowel *surgery*."

I glance at the computer monitor, to which the specialty list is taped. There's nothing about surgery beneath Dr. Jack Patrick's name. Only something about hepatic and pancreatic cancer.

So, I turn back to Joel and apologize, deciding to let it go instead of being the immature orderly who'd whine, "*But, no one ever tooooold me!*"

"One more thing—the top shelf of each person's box is for regular mail, the second is for internal mail, and the third is for appointment requests. Don't just stick everything in the top."

Again, this is news to me.

"When *you* make mistakes, *I'm* the one who looks bad." Joel's arms fold.

I apologize once more, promising it won't happen again. I think my relenting behavior takes him by surprise; his face softens.

"No one's mad or anything," he spurts with a shrug. Right. Dr. Stuart yells because he's *not* mad. Of course. "And, it's no big deal. I mean, it *is* a big deal, but because you're new, it's not… if that makes sense."

I assure him that it does make plenty of sense, then I take my seat.

The mail arrives an hour later. For the first time, Joel sits beside me and helps me sort, explaining every special exception not mentioned on the department list.

* * *

By mid-January, Jim and I successfully made up GI-related nicknames for everyone in the Department of Bowel Diseases. We never use these epithets in their presence, of course, though it's hard not to slip. Dr. Stuart is The Stool. Isabella Bethany Smith, a secretary, is Irritable Bowel Syndrome—or IBS, for short. John Cole is John Cholera. Dr. Patrick is Dr. Peptic-Ulcer. Colin was Colon—that was easy. And, of course, Joel Ilea and Mary Ceco where The Ileum and The Cecum.

I had to find *some* way to stay entertained, after all. I've been here after school every day for 2 straight weeks, and all I've ever done so far is run the front desk. I always arrive hopeful that I'd be sent to Radiology. But, instead, it's all phones and faxes and patient sign-ins, throughout the afternoon and evening. I want to see some real medical stuff. Watch some doctors at work, deliberating pictures of peculiar barium clouds. I didn't come all the way to the hospital to answer phones and sort mail.

Yesterday, Dr. Stuart published an article railing against the SCHIP bill—a controversial piece of legislation that proposes raising tobacco taxes to fund children's healthcare. It's being debated in Congress at this very moment. Right off the bat, the bill sounded like a good idea to me, but no one's really interested in what a 17-year-old orderly has got to say. The Stool is the official voice of the hospital. He believes that the smoking population in America is too small to financially sustain a program like that.

The phone rings.

I snatch up the receiver. "Good afternoon, Department of Bowel Diseases, how may I help you?"

"Yes," a man's voice sounds on the line, "I'd like to know if Dr. Stuart has children?"

What a random question. "Um, yes, sir, he does…"

"Well," the man's tone turns testy, "I hope that they all get sick one day and are unable to find healthcare!" And, with that, he hangs up with a spectacular bang.

Almost instantly, the phone rings again.

"I find his point-of-view quite literally nauseating," a woman croaks, not bothering to introduce herself either. *Nauseating?* As serious as the SCHIP issue was, I must stifle a laugh. Her tone is so outrageous, it's cartoonish.

The next call is from a mother who wants an appointment *today* with The Stool. As the Chief, his waitlist is a mile long.

"My 6-year-old will just *die* if she isn't seen by Dr. Stuart, *right now!*" she wails, tearfully.

It's going to be a long afternoon.

* * *

In Civics class, we're reading this book called *Eyewitness to Power* by David Gergen, a journalist and political speechwriter who served under Richard Nixon. Gergen wrote all about how Nixon enshrouded himself in a 'realm of personal privacy,' carrying a 'big stick' and clinging to a 'madman theory of politics... cultivating an air of mystique... for if others thought he was tough, vindictive, even a little mad, they would more likely stay out of his way.'

Nixon didn't need a radiologist to diagnose *his* problem: he was clearly suffering from a severe confusion between *leadership* and *power*. Ideally, I think leaders should weave their subordinates' ideas into an intricate master plan. Leaders should bring their underlings along willingly, working toward a common goal. The relationship between leader and follower is meant to be one of sharing, of giving and taking. Raw power, on the other hand, is a force of sheer control. Power does not ask nor guide, it demands and drags. It doesn't bother to accept input or share its own thoughts and speculations. It rules by fear and intimidation.

Though the comparison may be a little extreme, I think a parallel can be drawn between Nixon's leadership system and that of the Nation's Capital Bowels. And, it is The Stool who functions as Nixon in this paradigm.

Although he teaches classes and cures people for a living, I've come to discover that The Stool isn't a people-person in the least. Sometimes, I wonder why in the world he decided to become a doctor. I don't think that an interest in medical science is really enough to pick that career path. I think you have to actually *like* humanity before de-ciding to make a career out of saving lives. Sick patients aren't just regular folks, after all—they're in *pain*, which means they're not going to be all sunshine and rainbows when they come to see you. They're going to whine and cry and snap. And, as a medical professional, you're supposed to take it all in stride, understanding where they're coming from. If your internal reaction to a sick guy's complaint is 'when's lunch?' then you're not cut out to be a physician, even if you can recite the periodic table backward in your sleep.

When not seeing patients or giving lectures, Dr. Stuart sits with his office door not just closed, but locked. And, almost every single call for him gets sent to voicemail.

"Doctor," I tell him now, over the phone, "on the line, we have Mr. Mark Ernst from the Informed Consent Initiative, answering your email about scheduling a seminar for your residents."

"What in the world is the Informed Consent Initiative?" The Stool barks at me. Wait, what? Mark's claiming that Dr. Stuart answered *his* message. Yet, the doctor doesn't even know what the man's organization is *about?* "Ask him!"

"One moment please," I say, pushing LINE.

"Sir," I address Mark, wondering how I could word this without offending, "The

Sto—Dr. Stuart would like you to… um… clarify the purpose of your organization?"

There's a stunned silence. "But, he wrote me earlier today," he pipes. "He should know who we are!"

Helpless, I switch back. "Would you quit bothering me!" he yells. "Put him to my voicemail!"

Sheesh, imagine being his patient.

BLANCA ROKITANSKY

I hate cold weather, but I guess if I have to pick between winter and summer, I'd pick winter. I've never been able to eat much—tummy's too small—so, I don't really have any natural insulation. But, my skin can hardly take a photon of sunlight, so I'm stuck inside most of the summer. When I *do* have to go out, I must wear long sleeves and pants, no matter how hot. And, I carry an umbrella because a wide-brimmed hat, sunglasses and SPF 70 aren't always enough to properly shield me. At least, in the winter, overdressing doesn't look strange.

But, now, winter's over. It's a warm late-April morning. Adjusting my cap and prescription sunglasses, I run out to the bus-stop.

The great orange monster arrives only a minute later, and it's also full of monsters…

"Was that Blanca or just a puff of smoke?" says a tall blonde boy with a basketball, squinting about. I don't even know his name.

But, of course, he knows mine. Everyone does. He turns and shrugs dramatically to his friend—a shorter, smaller, African-American boy who's in my biology class. Russell Brown.

Russell doesn't seem amused.

"Hi, Blanca," he greets me with a mellow voice. His serene amber eyes—a touch lighter than his cinnamon skin—settle on mine, as though able to delineate my pink irises through my reflective shades. "How're you doing this morning?"

I look away. Russell isn't mean to me like the rest of my peers, but I hate that over-cautious voice he always uses with me. His tone gets all proper and official, like I'm his patient or something. 'Pre-pre-med,' he calls himself. I don't know why anyone would want to spend all those years studying and studying and studying just to wind up in a hospital for the rest of their lives. Hospitals are horrible places. If you don't *have* to go to one, don't go. Russell is crazy.

Wordlessly, I settle behind him and his obnoxious companion. I spend the rest of the ride listening to them talk about sports, watching the back of Russell's tightly-curled head. Soon enough, I find myself staring enviously at his honey-mocha skin, thinking about how unfair it is that some people have more than enough melanin to handle the summer sun and look nice and healthy and all lit up like that, while others have to be sickly and pale and forced to stay inside all the time.

* * *

District of Colombia High is really crowded. Crowded and poorly-designed. All the lockers are aligned in massive rows of 40 in the center of the building, instead of up against the wall like a normal well-funded school with space to spare. My last name, being neither at the beginning of the alphabet nor the end, got me assigned to a locker right in the dead center of the tenth row. So, several times a day, every day, I have to push and shove and get trampled just to swap out my books or grab my lunch-bag.

It doesn't help that everyone is just so much *bigger* than me. I've always been the smallest kid in class. I never understood why, since my parents are both average-sized. I don't have any brothers or sisters to compare myself to, because after giving birth to a colorless freak like me, my mom and dad decided that they didn't want any more children.

Relatively, I have long legs and a short torso. All my height is in my legs. My limbs are like popsicle-sticks, except not as dark, bubbling out at the joints. And, my skin stretches tightly across my abdomen and ribcage, like someone inside me is running a vacuum-cleaner against the walls of my flesh. Sometimes, I look at my midsection in the mirror and wonder how all the organs actually fit in there. Maybe, they're all smushed up against each other.

When I was in middle-school, a girl in my locker-row told me that, when I turn to the side, I look like I'm disappearing.

"You're so flat, so tiny," she squeaked, smacking bright-pink bubblegum. "When you turn, it's like you're vanishing!"

She was the first peer to ever call me a 'ghost.' So small and pale, I could just float away, or become invisible. I wish. I attract attention wherever I go. So *not* like being invisible.

"Lookathagirl," a random boy now gawks as I pass him in the corridors. "She's, what, 12?"

That's another thing: everyone here thinks I'm younger than I am. I'm 17, like most of the seniors. But, people often ask me if I skipped grades or something. I wish I did, so that way I'd have an easily-understood excuse for being so small. At least, there's a simple explanation for my pallor—I'm albino—but, I don't even know how to explain my littleness. It just is.

* * *

Like any kid, I love the way hot mozzarella strings trail from pizza slices when you take bites. I love the salty taste of french fries and how the crispiness turns to warm goo in your mouth when you chew. I like the creaminess of custard and how it slips down your throat. But, after the fun part— the biting and chewing and swallowing— it's always downhill from there. I get lots of tummy cramps. So, though I'm thin as a rail, I have to watch what I eat. I don't buy lunch from the school cafeteria very often. I pack my own. And, it's always something boring like turkey sandwiches and apple slices. Most days, I can't even finish. But, I always try.

I used to be worse. Before my growth-spurt, hunger was a completely foreign sensation to me. My mom actually asked the elementary-school cafeteria janitor to keep an eye on me at lunch and call her if I threw anything away.

She just didn't understand. Still doesn't. No one really does. It's not that I don't *want* to eat more. It's that I can't. Because when I get full, I don't just feel bloated and uncomfortable for a little while, like normal people. Fullness for me has always entailed overbearing sharp pains below my gut—like someone is twisting my tummy with their bare hands—for hours on end. When I overeat, even by a couple bites, the ache strikes and sometimes doesn't leave until the next day. So, I always have to stop eating when I'm just barely satisfied, not 'full.'

People like to comment on my food. "Always the same thing," they say. They don't realize that it's just safer this way, to eat what my gut is used to rather than playing with the fire of the unknown. I don't know why my stomach and I aren't friends, but as long as I stay obedient to its strict demands, it lets me stay alive.

*　*　*

The flu is going around. Lots of people are absent from school today, including both my lab partner and Russell's. So, the teacher matches us up.

I watch him unpack his bookbag slowly and methodically, honey-hand retrieving notebooks and pencils.

Russell always plays basketball straight through lunch-period and winds up trying to sneak food into bio. I think it's weird and kind of nasty to eat in the same room where fetal pigs and frogs are dissected, but it seems like Russell isn't grossed out by anything.

I watch him rip open a bag of corn chips, feeling a pang of envy. I can hardly remember the last time I ate something crunchy and orange that isn't a carrot-stick.

The teacher flicks off the lights and turns on the TV; I swap my prescription shades for regular glasses. It's a video on the human digestive system. The moment that becomes apparent, Russell just seems to light up. He sits straight as an arrow, mouth full, amber eyes wide. You'd think we're seeing Star Wars or something, not a dull film about bellies and bowels.

When Russell gets up from his chair to sharpen his pencil, I steal a chip from his bag. One taste can't hurt my tummy too bad, can it? That's what I always tell myself when serious urges strike.

Licking the glorious specs of dehydrated cheese from the roof of my mouth, I watch as the video opens. Soon, it's a struggle just to keep my *eyes* open. We have an exam coming up soon in which we'll have to label a diagram of the gastrointestinal tract, describing what all the parts do. But, honestly, I can care less about the difference between gallbladders and gut-blubber. As I begin to feel mildly nauseous, my enthusiasm for the subject diminishes all the more.

On the screen, the first segment of the small intestines illuminates. "This is called the duodenum," a monotonous voice blares, and I mechanically take notes. "It begins with the duodenal bulb directly below the stomach and ends with the suspensory muscle, known as the ligament of Treitz. Here, the digestive juices from the pancreas and liver mix together and…"

I rub my tummy with my left hand, right where I imagine my duodenum is. I close my eyes, feeling a bit woozy. Must be the chip.

"Are you okay?"

I open my eyes, startled to find Russell's russet-colored face only a couple inches from mine.

"Um, yeah," I murmur, startled. "I'm fine."

He doesn't break his stare. "You know, I don't think I've ever seen your eyes before," he comments, "since you're always wearing those shades."

I wait for the typical 'oh-my-gosh-they're-pink!' comment to come.

His gaze lingers on mine a moment longer. "I think they're pretty," he says in a matter-of-fact tone before popping another chip in his mouth and abruptly turning back to the film.

I feel my insides squirm, yet again. Nausea never felt so pleasant.

BLANCA ROKITANSKY

I knew all along that it's only a matter of time. I knew there's no way the flu could go around the school without eventually hitting me. Sure enough, I'm coming down with a sore throat and fever.

I don't exactly have friends at District of Colombia High, so it's daunting to skim the DCHS directory to figure out who to call to ask about homework.

I pick Russell.

"Missed you at school, today," he says in his doctor-voice. "Everything okay?"

I yank the curly phone-cord, which reminds me of Russell's corkscrewed hair. "I have the flu."

"I'm sorry to hear that. I know you weren't feeling well in bio, yesterday."

"No, that's unrelated. That was belly pain. Today is mostly a head-nose-throat kind of thing." Ugh, why did I say that? I just want to get my homework assignments and hang up, as quickly as possible.

"Unrelated?" He sounds much too curious. Damn my loose lips. "What was going on, then?"

Why does it matter? "I don't know," I shrug, "maybe, something I ate." I thought about the single stolen chip, fingers drumming against the kitchen table. "Anyway, I'm calling to ask about homework. Anything new?"

"Not really. Just the same stuff that's been assigned for a while now. The civics paper on Gergen's book is due Monday, and the biology exam on the digestive system is on Wednesday."

I shuffle through my backpack. I haven't even started studying for the bio test yet.

"Shoot, I left my bio book at school."

In DC, that's a much bigger deal than it sounds. The metro doesn't run through this area, and by car, 4 miles is liable to take 40 minutes. Not that I even had a car. I couldn't ask my parents, either: my mom pulls the evening shift at a supermarket and my dad is constantly away on business trips. He works for the CIA. Right now, he's somewhere in

Asia (or, so he says), probably doing something dangerous and top-secret.

"Want to borrow mine?" Russell asks, taking me by surprise. "I can bring it over. We live far closer to each other than either of us do to the school."

I shift the phone to my other ear. "Don't *you* need it to study?"

"I'll be over in 10 minutes." He hangs up.

10 minutes.

I sprint to the bathroom, snatch off my shades and anxiously peer at my reflection. A runny nose and fever don't exactly compliment a girl's looks. There's dried mucus below my left nostril, dark circles around my eyes, and dewy perspiration at my hairline. My PJs are faded and wrinkled and damp with sweat.

Unfortunately, there's no time to shower. I quickly wash my face, brush my teeth and run a comb through my limp white locks. I hate how my hair lies so flat on my head, as though permanently plastered down by all the hats I always have to wear. I pull a clump of hair off the comb and toss it in the trash. It resembles a knot of spiderweb.

I sprint to my room, throwing off my pajamas. I wad them into a ball and hurl them in my closet, then hastily put on a blue button-down and a pair of beige cargos. The fashion these days is the 'skinny' pant, but on me it looks way *too* skinny, so I always opt for something baggier. I barely have time to pull on a pink scrunchie when the doorbell rings. I scurry downstairs, wearing my regular glasses rather than my shades. If Russell thinks my eyes are pretty, I don't want to hide them.

I yank the door open.

"Hey, Blanca." Russell grins his dimpled grin, which makes me think of ripples in freshly-stirred coffee.

"Hey," I breathe. "Thanks for bringing your book." I reach for it.

To my astonishment, he doesn't hand it over, but invites himself in.

"I figure we can study together for a bit, before I give up my book entirely," he chuckles, unzipping his backpack. "Sound good?"

I blink, now wishing that I *did* wear my sunglasses so he wouldn't see the surprise in my eyes. "Um, yeah, sure, that'd be great… but, I'm probably contagious…"

Russell laughs heartily, at this. "Oh, Blanca, Blanca." My stomach flutters as he repeats my name. "The flu has been preventable for some time, now. I've been vaccinated. Not to mention, I generally never get sick."

"Oh. Well, okay, then." My voice comes out flat. Ugh, this is my first time having a kid over from school—my first chance to maybe make a real friend. But, instead of being cheerful and grateful and showing some personality, I'm acting all evasive and dull.

He settles at the kitchen table, skin matching the wooden chair. "Why didn't you get a flu shot?" he asks oh-so-casually, turning to the chapter on the digestive system.

I shrug. "I've known a lot of people who actually *got* the flu from a flu shot." And, considering my luck, I always figured I'd be among them if I ever got vaccinated myself.

"That's only possible if the culture is 'live' instead of 'dead,'" he says, getting all doctorly on me. "The live ones are more effective, but they also carry a slight risk of making those with weaker immune systems sick. So, you still had another option."

What? "I've never heard of live versus dead cultures before. I thought all flu vaccines are the same."

"Your general practitioner never told you?" he gasps, scandalized.

"Um, no…" Why does he care? "I think we should start studying, now."

Russell isn't listening. "Who's your GP, anyway?"

A slippery white lock escapes from my scrunchie and flops before my glasses. I flick it behind my ear. "What?"

"Do you go to Nation's Capital Teaching Hospital?" he presses.

"That's none of your business," I find myself saying, to my astonishment.

He looks away.

"Let's study," I repeat, sheepishly.

Russell positions the book exactly in the middle of the space between us, on the table. Seems fair, right? Except that my sight isn't 20-20, even with glasses. (Without, I'm legally blind). So, the only words I can see now are those on the rightward page—the page closest to me. But, I'm too shy to say anything or pull the book closer.

After about 10 minutes, Russell's head pops up. "How 'bout we quiz each other?"

I don't think I'm ready to be drilled yet, but I say yes anyway.

"Great. I'll test you first." He drags the book away from me, as to prevent me from peeking. Like I could. "What does the pancreas do?"

Shoot, that one wasn't on my side. "Um… make bile?"

"Close, but no. The pancreas *does* produce a variety of digestive juices, but not bile— that's the liver." Damn him; he's not even looking at the text as he says this.

"Oh. What's the difference between bile and pancreatic juice?"

He grins. "No, no, I'm the one testing *you*."

I really wish I weren't so fair; I can never get away with embarrassment. My face always glows like a stoplight. Sure enough, his eyes now flicker to my flaming cheeks.

Good going, Blanca. Total idiocy is always a great way to impress a biology whiz. Well, I can't help it if my stronger area is English literature. At 17, I've already had poetry and short stories published in professional literary magazines, but heaven forbid, I don't find human bowels interesting. Why do we have to wait until college to start specializing? I shouldn't have to waste my time with medical mumbo-jumbo when I already know I want to be a novelist, not a biologist. Who *cares* what the pancreas does?

"Bile only breaks down fatty acids," Russell finally explains, "but, pancreatic excretion breaks down fats, carbohydrates *and* proteins."

Fatty acids. That phrase sounds so funny. It's weird, to think of fats as acids. When I hear the word 'fat,' I imagine a tub of margarine, or a stick of butter, or a squirt of icing. Creamy and smooth, not acidic. It won't burn your mouth like lemons or onions—foods that *do* come to mind when I think of 'acid.'

And, now, I'm picturing a pretty pink, fluffy, frosted birthday cake, burning a hole through the table. Cake. Gosh, I can't even remember the last time I ate cake.

"Blanca?" Russell waves a butterscotch hand at me. "Earth to Blanca!"

"What? Oh, sorry." The pink cake abruptly vanishes. "Sorry, I guess all this digestive-system stuff is making me think about food," I laugh, stupidly.

"Are you hungry?"

I shrug.

"'Cause, if you are, I brought something." He reaches into his backpack and pulls out a family-sized bag of corn chips. Dammit. "Want some?" He pops it open. "You look like you could do with some food." I note his word-choice. *You look like you could do with some food.* It's not a friendly offer, but a prescription.

Despite myself, I reach in and grab a handful. I shove a couple seasoned triangles into my mouth. "Ask me another question," I say, crunching.

"Okay." Russell gives me a confused grin. "What does the gallbladder do?"

I don't know the answer, so I shove another chip into my mouth to buy time.

"Here's a hint—it's related to the other question we were discussing, a second ago."

I swallow. "Bile?"

He nods. "What about bile?"

I nibble the corner of a fourth chip. "It stores bile?"

"Right! Now, under what conditions will the gallbladder contract and push the bile into the small intestines?"

I lick dehydrated cheese from my lips. "When a person eats fats."

"Right again." He pushes the book toward me. "Now, you quiz me a bit."

"Sure." Studying has never been so fun. I look down at the text, figuring I should give him a tough one since he probably already knows it all. "What's the name of the first portion of the small intestine," I read carefully, "that's responsible for the initial breakdown of food using enzymes?"

Suddenly, I feel as though a giant snake is hatching inside my gut. Out of nowhere, it writhes and thrashes—my belly makes a loud noise, like the inaugural crack of a thunderstorm. I jump from my chair. There's no time to make it to the bathroom, so I have to do the unthinkable: I puke in the kitchen sink, right in front of Russell.

I lift my head from the drain, horrified to find Russell out of his seat, standing *directly* over me. Oh, my gosh. He's looking right at *it!*

"I-I'm so sorry," I babble, sleeve-wiping my mouth. The *one* time I have a friend over from school, and look what I do! I *know* I can't tolerate fried foods—why did I let my guard down *today,* of all days? I turn on the faucet, and the vivid orange goo breaks into lumpy amber.

"There's no need to apologize," he says mildly. "Are you okay?"

I wave my hand. "Oh, sure," I lie, gut still thrashing. "It's probably just my flu, you know."

"But, you said yours is more of a 'head-nose-throat' kind of thing,'" he objects. "You never said anything about your stomach."

"Oh, um… well, I guess my tummy is bit upset, too."

"Since when?"

I look away. "Since always," I murmur.

"What?"

I shrug. "I'm going to go brush my teeth, then we can continue."

He blinks. "You want to keep studying? I think you should rest."

"Oh, come on, this is nothing—it happens *all* the time."

His eyes turn to yellow traffic-lights. "It *does?*"

His cell phone, sitting on the table, suddenly lights up and belts:

"I wanna heal,
I wanna feel,

Like I'm close to something real,
I wanna find something I've wanted all
aloooooong,
SOMEWHERE I BELOOOOOONG!"

"Linkin Park," I recognize. "That's a good song. From *Hybrid Theory,* right?"

He nods, a slight pink twinge touching his dimpled cheeks as he silences Chester Bennington in mid-cry. Why would Russell pick that specific song? Sure, it has a strong beat and a great melody... but, the words. The words describe someone who's been wounded, alienated. And, Bennington's voice, like poisoned caramel, imbues those words with even more tragic power.

"I have to go. My sister said she'd call me when she's out of swim-team practice; I need to pick her up."

There are hours until my mom—the only other member of the Rokitansky family in the US at the moment—comes home from work. And, now, Russell has to leave, too. Well, at least, I won't have to face any more of his pre-pre-med inquiries, for now. Saved by the bell.

He swings his backpack over his shoulder. "Mind if I call you sometime, to check up on you?"

Not so he could *chat* with me, but so he could *check up* on me. The doctor-thing, again! But, even so, I'm thrilled. A kid from school wants to call me. I didn't scare him off with the whole barfing thing.

"Sure," I breathe.

"Great." He zips up and marches to the door. Then, he suddenly turns and spouts, "Duodenum."

I blink. "What?"

"Duodenum," he repeats. "It's the answer to the question you just asked me—what's the first part of the small intestines."

I glance down at the book, and sure enough, he's right. When I peer back up, he's gone.

I lay my hands on the part that hurts, the part right below my belly.

Duodenum.

RUSSELL BROWN

Blanca is yet to return to school. It's Friday. She missed the test on Wednesday. I called her that night, but her mother said she was asleep. I called her on Thursday evening, but no one picked up.

I open my front door now, having just driven back from the metro. Commuting is quite an ordeal, even though both my home and the hospital are in the same city. Unfortunately, when that city is DC, it can require 3+ forms of transportation to get somewhere only 5 miles away. My trip is particularly complicated by a few fun factors: 1) there's no metro-stop within walking distance of my apartment complex, so I have to drive to the Metro Center and spend 20 minutes trying to hunt down a parking space; 2) the hospital can't spare an employee parking slot for a lowly high-school orderly and the patient lot costs $25 a day, which is out-of-the question for a kid working a volunteer job, and 3) believe it or not, Nation's Capital University does not have its own metro-stop—in fact, the nearest one to the college campus is in Virginia. No joke. The University is located just off the Key Bridge. So, to get to work, I take the Orange Line to Rosslyn (in Arlington, Virginia) where, thankfully, the university sends a shuttle. The shuttle, which runs only once every half-hour, takes me to the undergrad campus, where I get off and walk all the way to the medical grounds. This whole rigmarole takes over an hour, and the funny thing is, I could probably see my apartment building out the window of the surgical center inpatient tower.

Today, Joel Ilea let me work in the Radiology Department for the first time since fake-interview-day. I spent my entire shift, right there with the technicians and patients, watching everything. It was what I've wanted since my internship began.

My shift kicked off with a 40-year-old woman getting a computed tomography scan of her abdomen and pelvis. As the technician began to prep her IV contrast solution, I gave her a pair of 16-ounce barium sulfate bottles to down at a rate of 8 ounces every 15 minutes.

"This stuff tastes horrible," she gagged. "It's like liquid chalk."

I peered inside the bottle, at the lumpy white liquid. It smelled rank, like rotten apples and urine. Chalk was probably a generous comparison. Involuntarily, I shuddered. It seemed cruel and ironic that, in order to diagnose, we must force sick people to drink something that'd make even the healthiest person want to hurl.

"Russell," said the tech, a middle-aged man named Mark. "Could you open the second drawer over there and fetch an informed-consent form? The one that's in the third file, for intravenous contrast dye."

Funny he should ask that *after* starting the IV-drip. It was like were only pretending to get her consent. I retrieved the form:

'Patients should inform the radiologist or technologist if they have a history of allergies (especially to medications, previous iodine injections or shellfish), diabetes, asthma, heart conditions, kidney problems or thyroid conditions. These conditions may

indicate a higher risk of iodine reactions or problems with eliminating the substance after the exam. The most common side effect of iodine includes hot flashes, a metallic taste in the mouth and heat in the bladder area. Following the administration of iodine, patients may experience itching over various parts of the body with hives (bumps on the skin). This reaction can last from several minutes to several hours. More serious reactions, although less likely, may include difficulty breathing, swelling of the throat or swelling of other parts of the body. These reactions can be harmful or fatal if not treated immediately—'

"Russell," Mark barked. "I think the patient needs it, not you."

"Oh, sorry," I breathed sheepishly, handing it over.

Seconds later, she sheet was signed and the patient was flat on her back, sliding into the whirring tube. Mark and I stepped into an adjoining observation room. I watched as he put on a headset and pushed a few buttons.

"Hold your breath," he told her through the intercom. A few seconds later, he ordered, "Now, breathe."

The pattern repeated itself for 20 minutes: hold your breath—now, breathe—hold your breath, again—and breathe—hold your breath—hey, don't move!

On the screen before us, milky-grey shapes swam in a sea of black. It didn't look anything like what I imagined when I thought of abdomens. I saw a series of lopsided grey ovals, each containing lots of white and black squiggles and dots.

Mark noticed the confusion on my face. "It's a cross-section," he explained, "like a sliced loaf of bread." He pointed to the dark mass in the middle. "This is her stomach." His finger slid to the rippled grey tube. "Those are her intestines." He indicated the brightest white dot. "And, that's her spine."

A cross-section. I was beginning to get it, now. It was as though I were floating directly above the patient, looking straight down. What an awkward angle.

"Wouldn't it be easier to take shots from the front?" I asked. "Everything is so compact, like this."

"What you're describing is an Upper-GI series, not a CT," he said. "A UGI would provide great images, sure, but it also takes a lot longer to administer. The patient would be here for at least 2 hours, imaged every 15 minutes as the barium travels farther down her digestive tract. We tend only to only use UGIs to verify a diagnosis already made from a CT." He expanded a window on the screen. "In minutes, a CT gives you dozens of pictures, 'slice' by 'slice,' that can be played back like a movie."

At the end of the test, the technician ran the video from beginning to end, smoothly. It looked like white noodles squirming inside an undulating grey dish. It took all of 30 seconds.

"That's it?" My brows lifted.

He nodded. "Most of the time, this is all a radiologist needs to make a diagnosis."

"Wow," I breathed, watching the patient slide out of the tube. "Well, I hope they find out what's wrong with her."

Mark shrugged. "I'm not a doctor, but I've seen so many of these, I can usually tell when something's off. Her scan is fine."

"Oh." I frown. "So, what's causing her pain, then?"

He shrugged, again. "Like I said, I'm not a doctor. But, I'd be willing to bet that she just has IBS."

IBS. Irritable Bowel Syndrome. Oh yes, I'd heard of *that* before. That's what my mom was (mis)diagnosed with before she died of Crohn's Disease when I was 10. IBS is very common... and incurable. Causes abdominal pain, indigestion, nausea, constipation and/or diarrhea, along with a variety of other unpleasant symptoms that tend to vary pretty widely from person to person. A 'functional' disorder, it's called. Doesn't show up on x-rays nor blood-tests nor biopsies nor any other exam, for that matter. It's supposed to be a 'diagnosis of exclusion' because most other conditions *do* show up on one test or another. I wondered at that moment if IBS is so 'common' because it's inaccurately over-diagnosed, since it sure would require a whole truckload of exams to rule out *every*thing else that overlaps with the too-wide and vague umbrella of 'IBS symptoms.' Not to mention, it's incurable, so handing out a diagnosis of IBS lets the doctors off easy: from then on, they have no responsibility to cure you, only to help 'manage' your pain—basically, they tell you to go take gas-control meds and avoid about 75% of the food pyramid since, for reasons unknown, it all makes you sick. Telling someone with abdominal pain that they have IBS is basically like informing someone with a sore leg that they have Sore Leg Syndrome.

I thought about this the entire drive home from the metro, sitting in traffic. I wondered if that woman was ever going to get any answers or if she was going to fall prey to the popular IBS condemnation.

Now, I'm standing in the kitchen, munching corn chips, which of course turns my thoughts to Blanca and her puking and her never-ending flu. Washing down the cheesy dust with a swig of cherry-cola, I yank the cordless phone off the wall and punch in Blanca's number, which I've memorized by now since I've been trying to get a hold of her all week.

Lo and behold, someone actually answers: "Hello?" Her voice comes out small and weak.

"Blanca," I plunk down my can, "it's Russell. Did I wake you up?"

There's a short pause. "Oh, no, not at all." She sounds surprised. "Good to hear from you. How are you?"

How am *I?* "How about you answer that question first?" I say, maybe a little too harshly.

"Oh, um," she hesitates, "I'm getting better, slowly but surely."

"Getting better how?" I persist. "Like your throat, fever and sinuses?"

"Yeah. Flu's almost gone."

"What about your stomach?"

Silence.

"Blanca?"

"My stomach's... well, I mean, it's... it's always been..."

"Always been what?"

Another pause.

"I'm fine, really." She sounds flustered.

"Doesn't sound like you're fine. Maybe, there's something else going on, besides the flu."

"Russell," her tone drops a couple octaves, "you're not my doctor. You're not *a* doctor."

"I know, but—"

She sighs directly into the receiver—a sharp, angry wind whips my ear. "I've always had a weak tummy, okay? So, what's happening now isn't as strange as you think it is, not for me. My tummy has always been irritable. It just gets a little worse after other illnesses, sometimes."

"What kind of illnesses?"

"Like this flu. And, when I had sinusitis, last month."

"But, *why?*" I breathe. "Sinusitis has got nothing to do with the GI system. Why should that make your belly upset?"

BLANCA ROKITANSKY

"I don't know why," I growl to Russell, over the phone. "I don't even know why we're having this conversation."

This was going beyond the realm of 'concerned friend.' Russell was playing doctor with me. He was getting a kick out of diving into a medical mystery. Blanca, the strange little albino girl who has strange things wrong with her body. So, allow me, Mr. Healthy Athlete, to be all philanthropic and doctorly, sticking my nose in her private business. Russell and I only 'hung out' once before; our relationship is so premature, I don't know if it even qualifies as friendship. He's an acquaintance. And, I don't share gristly medical details with acquaintances.

"I-I'm sorry," Russell sputters, "I don't mean to be rude. I'm just worried about you; I want to help."

"Well, there's no need to worry," I find myself blurting. "I've been dealing with GI issues my whole life and no doctor has been able to figure it out so I don't think some pre-pre-med high-schooler stands a chance. And, apparently, I've managed to live with my stomach for 17 years just fine, so—"

"Sure, you are," Russell's voice slices through mine, "for now. But, the bottom line is, something isn't right. You're still young; things may be manageable *now*, but one of these days they might just spiral out of control and blow up in your face, then what will you do? I don't know what disease you have, but early detection is—"

What *disease* I have? "I'm not *diseased!*" I cry. "That's just the way my stomach *works!*"

"Or, *not* works," he snorted. "Blanca, don't you want to know how it feels to *not* live in pain? To eat whatever you want, unconcerned with nausea or vomiting? Don't you want to be able to go out to dinner without having to worry about every single ingredient in your meal, or if your seat is near enough to the restroom for you to be able to run over in time? You don't *have* to live like this. I don't know why so many patients choose to live in pain, ignoring it for years and years until, all of a sudden, they find themselves bedridden in the hospital with some ghastly final-stage diagnosis, wondering how in the world they got to that point."

There's a pause. I swallow, lost for words.

Russell exhales. "People always say, 'I never saw it coming,' but the truth is, they did. They just chose to turn a blind eye. They let things build up instead of taking care of it when it was only a nuisance."

I sit on the floor, chest to my knees. That position always helps to calm my nausea a little. No idea why.

"You don't understand, Russell," I finally speak. "It's not that I haven't been checked out, before. My mom and I tried, many years ago, when I was 8. The doctors just weren't able to find anything. One day, after months and months of appointments that went nowhere, one of them finally told me, 'your stomach's just weak; probably IBS,' and we left it at that. We figured, since it's manageable and not life-threatening, it's not such a big deal."

"Well, I think you should try again. Get a second opinion."

I snort.

"Okay, maybe, it's more like a zillionth opinion—whatever," Russell sighs. "You shouldn't settle for a diagnosis like IBS until *everything else* has been ruled out."

"That could take forever," I breathe. "I could probably live in the hospital for ages before everything gets ruled out. I mean, if I do have something else, it's definitely uncommon—not Celiac's nor Crohn's nor H. Pylori—because I've already been tested for all that stuff. I think the only things left are those super rare conditions that only happen on TV or in the movies," I chuckle. "I mean, what are the odds of something like *that?*"

He gives a dry laugh. "Look who's talking. Chances of albinism are, what, 1:10,000?"

"17,000," I correct.

"Well, then, you should know better than anyone that rare things don't just happen to *other* people."

I rub my temples.

"Call your GP. Tell him you want to start over. Get referred to a specialist, and begin getting tested. Be sure to let them know if anything's changed since last time."

"Last time?"

"When you were 8. Are your symptoms now *exactly* the same as then?"

"Not quite…" I yank the curly phone-cord.

"How so?"

I lie down completely on the floor now, on my left side, and speak barely above a whisper: "To be perfectly honest… these days, I can hardly swallow a bite without feeling sick. I don't mean that figuratively. I mean, a bite of *anything*. Rice. Dry bread. A cracker. Doesn't matter what it is. I used to only respond poorly to heavier things, like fried food and desserts. Like your chips. But, now, it just takes one nibble of even the blandest thing to set me off." I inhale. "Sometimes, I don't even have to eat for it to hurt." Like, right now. "It just amps up, overwhelming me, for no reason at all. It feels like… twisting, stabbing."

It feels so wrong, so dangerous, to be telling all this to a boy from school. A boy I don't even know very well. I mean, I *think* Russell is trustworthy, but for all I know, he could turn right around and tell everyone at DCHS on Monday what a freak I am.

"Okay," Russell says, absorbing my confessional like a professional. "The moment we hang up, I want you to call your doctor and schedule an appointment. Right now. Promise me you'll do that?"

"It's Friday night," I object.

"Right. Well, do it first thing Monday, okay?"

"I-I'll have to check in with my mom about her schedule, to see when she could drive me over there—I mean, she works a lot of hours and—"

"Just accept the next available appointment and *I'll* take you, if she can't."

I try to imagine walking into Nation's Capital Teaching Hospital with Russell, heading to the gastrointestinal unit they so obnoxiously named the 'Department of Bowel Diseases.' How mortifying.

"Oh, no," I breathe, "I wouldn't ask you to do that."

"I don't mind. I go to Nation's Capital all the time, anyway."

He does?

"Promise you'll schedule an appointment? For me?"

For *him?* For goodness' sake, maybe I do like his doctor-voice better than the syrupy overly-concerned-friend approach.

"Fine," I give in. "See you around."

"Bye, Blanca."

He hangs up.

From my spot on the floor, I look up at the phone receptacle, high on the wall. I pull myself into a sitting position, and immediately my gut begins to protest. Cold, sharp pain strikes directly below my stomach, like an icicle. Impaled, I slide back onto the frigid tile, clutching the receiver to my chest.

"*If you'd like to make a call, please hang up and try your call again. If you need help, hang up and then dial your operator,*" blares an automated voice from the receiver.

Minutes pass.

"*If you'd like to make a call, please hang up and try your call again. If you need help, hang up and then dial your operator,*" the robot-woman bellows again.

"I can't move," I pant, "or else I *would* hang up."

"*If you'd like to make a call, please hang up and try your call again. If you need help, hang up and then dial your operator.*"

"Please stop," I whimper.

"If you'd like to make a call, please hang up and try your call again. If you need help, hang up and then dial your operator."

"Shut up!" Imaginary fingers now throttle my gut, twisting, twisting, twisting—

"If you'd like to make a call, please hang up and try your call again. If you need help, hang up and then dial your operator."

"I said, SHUT UP!"

I picture my intestines thrashing like a snake while those iron hands mercilessly squeeze and pull and contort. I look down at my belly and gasp at the sight of a protrusion, right where the pain is. I rip open my shirt… revealing a terrifying golf-ball-sized lump, peeking below my ribcage.

Hysterical screams tear from my throat.

"If you'd like to make a call, please hang up and try your call again. If you need help, hang up and then dial your operator."

BLANCA ROKITANSKY

The hospital looks so dumpy from the outside. A combination of graffitied mud-brown bricks and stained concrete, punctured with the occasional foggy window. *This* is one of the top medical centers in America?

Today, July 25th, I'm supposed to see one of the top *doctors* in America. Dr. Benjamin Stuart of the Nation's Capital Department of Bowel Diseases.

I have good health insurance. Children of CIA agents tend to. With my coverage, I didn't need to get a referral from a general practitioner to see a specialist. So, the Monday after that chilling phone conversation with Russell, I called Nation's Capital and requested an appointment with a gastroenterologist directly.

"Ask to see the Chief of the Department," my mom insisted. "We're not wasting our time with any *tonto* like before!"

The lady on the phone took down my name, birthdate, guarantor, insurance provider, insurance group number, social security number and a few other such invasive facts that would fully enable the hospital to steal my identity in a heartbeat if they so desired.

"Alright, our next available appointment is July 25th," the scheduler finally said, after the interrogation was complete.

"July?" I echoed. It was late-April. "That's 3 months away."

"That's Dr. Stuart's next available appointment," she snapped, "take it or leave it."

"I'll take it," I sighed.

The next day at school, I told Russell. To my surprise, he didn't seem surprised.

"Dr. Stuart is on the national top-10 list," he said with a shrug. "That wait is actually shorter than average, to see someone like him. He's crazy-busy, not just with patients, but attending conventions, holding conferences, commuting between his fellowships at other hospitals, writing and publishing research papers, lecturing med classes— basically, doing far more that the average doc. His secretaries practically have secretaries of their own, and his appointment waiting-list goes on for a mile." He yanked one of his corkscrew-curls and it bounced back spectacularly. "Your 3-month wait must be a 'first-time patient special' or something. The problem is, I really don't think it's a good idea for *you* to hold off that long. A lot can happen in 3 months."

"I've lasted 17 years so far, Russell." I blinked, taken aback by his doomsday attitude. "I'm sure I can make it through 3 months."

He was silent.

After bio class ended, he slung his backpack over his shoulder and came straight to my desk. "Blanca," he said rather suddenly, as I zipped my own bag, "could you do me a favor?"

I looked up into his anxious amber eyes, reflecting patches of gold in the fluorescent lighting. "Of course," I spurted.

"I know I'm not your doctor—or, anybody's doctor, for that matter," he echoed my acidic words from the previous Friday, "but, could you please let me know right away if, when, and how your symptoms progress? You know, like, if anything changes or gets worse?"

Not 'let me know how you're doing' but 'let me know how your *symptoms progress.*' His word-choice reinforced that I wasn't, in fact, dealing with a friend, but someone who saw me as a patient. A science-project. A mystery to solve.

I looked away. "Sure," I said, blandly.

In my peripheral vision, I thought I saw little smile dimples appear on his cheeks. "Thanks, man."

And, with that, he disappeared out the door and joined up with his basketball teammates. His *real* friends.

* * *

April and May dissolved in a whirlwind of essays, presentations, final exams, stomach pains… and lots and lots of colds.

It seemed as though I was catching one every other week. And, with each, my appetite diminished all the more. My lunchtime turkey sandwich and apple soon became just a turkey sandwich. Then, half a turkey sandwich. Then, a couple bites of turkey sandwich.

Soon, I couldn't eat lunch at all. It was like breakfast sat in my belly all day like an anchor. My stomach would make thunderstorm-like noises after every meal and the little golf-ball would rise and fall as I struggled to hold back tears. After meals at home, I'd lie on the floor, on my left side, in the fetal position.

Since I couldn't exactly recline in the school cafeteria, I always tried to placate my gut's anger at lunch with its second-favorite position: leaning forward, chest to my knees, as though bowing in submission to its wrath.

June 1st arrived in a burst of glorious summer heat but terrible summer sunlight. The commencement ceremony was held in the schoolyard at noon that day, and even though the graduates had to wear long, flowing robes and wide mortar boards, I knew there was no way I could sit outside for so many hours, no matter what. And so, I lathered on several ounces of SPF 70—until my eyes stung and watered—and went out *just* long enough to dart across the stage, grab my diploma, shake the principal's hand, and zip back inside.

After the ceremony, I went out with Russell's family for a celebratory dinner at a steakhouse in Arlington. My dad was still in Asia and my mom had to race off to work, so I was the only Rokitansky in the group. And, I was nervous as hell. I'd agreed to go much earlier on in the year, before my stomach got *this* bad. By graduation day, I'd grown quite nervous about eating even a few bites in public because I never knew how my gut would react.

I sat down across from Russell at the long table, heavy with shiny silverware and orange candles and little glasses that looked like Christmas bulbs balancing on skinny crystal necks. I caught my reflection in the back of my spoon, and saw that in the dim light of the restaurant, my complexion wasn't so pasty. If I squinted my eyes or lowered my glasses, my reflection almost looked honeyed. I smiled.

"I can't believe high school is over," Russell interrupted my thoughts, looking rather scholarly in his robes and honor-society cords. "Congrats, Valedictorian!"

My smile slipped a little as I fiddled with my golden medallion. "It would've been nice to give a speech or something, like I was supposed to," I murmured.

"The Salutatorian did an okay job, I think," he said with a wink, stroking his silver medal.

I took a sip of water, and the icy liquid pelted my stomach as though I'd swallowed a hunk of raw beef—not a good omen for the food to come. I opened the menu and began to scan for an option that would maybe cause only 3-4 hours of pain instead of 8-10. But, everything listed seemed to be marinated, marbled, spiced, sauced or fried.

Russell's eyes hovered over a photo of a half-pound hunk of pepper-speckled sirloin, dripping in its own juices. "I feel silly wearing the grad robe off-campus," he murmured, offhand.

I chuckled, "This coming from a guy who wears scrubs to work." He'd recently clued me in on his volunteer internship.

"I don't mind scrubs, really. They feel a lot like pajamas. How many people can say they sport PJs to the office?"

Maybe, I could ask the cook to hold the marinade on my order of grilled chicken and *not* soak the bread in a massive vat of olive oil. "When you're a doctor, you're going to have to wear a white coat."

His nose wrinkled. "Whoever thought up of the whole white coat thing has clearly never set foot in a hospital. I mean, physicians get splashed with barf, blood and feces on a daily basis, so—"

"Russell!" his little sister squeaked. "We're about to *eat!*"

He chortled, toying with his giant steak-knife. "Sorry, I guess I've been desensitized."

I shivered, mind involuntarily conjuring a ghastly image of Russell holding an enormous surgical scalpel while dressed in a white coat so splattered with gore, it looked as though he'd been rolling around in a pile of fresh corpses.

The bistro steadily became more and more crowded—mostly with District of Colombia High graduates and their families—until the place was positively sweltering with body heat. Even *I* got warm enough to shed my gown. The blouse I wore underneath clung tightly to my damp skin.

When the food arrived, Russell sliced his steak slowly and methodically, like a surgeon making the first incision. I peered down at my plate, at the chunks of chicken breast that looked particularly dehydrated and sandy without the marinade, and the crusty white Kaiser roll in place of the restaurant's signature moist garlic bread.

I chewed a sliver of sandpaper-chicken as I watched Russell drench his steak in A1 sauce. As I swallowed, I felt the rubbery fibers scrape my throat.

"So, which summer orientation are you in?" he asked, mouth full. Russell and I were attending the same university this fall—Nation's Capital.

"Fourth. You?"

"First. Man, I love having a last name in the beginning of the alphabet."

I laboriously sawed my next bite of chicken. "I'm used to being next-to-last in everything. That's not always a bad thing, mind you, especially when it comes to things like class-project-presentation order, or something."

He chewed, face pensive. "So, what kind of name is Rokitansky anyway? Russian?"

"Czech."

He hummed. "It's really unusual. You could probably trace your genealogy pretty easily, with a name like that. As for me," he smirked, "I could be anyone from anywhere.

There are a lot of Browns. I don't even have a clue what country in Africa my ancestors are from, let alone who they were."

I took a crunchy bite of dinner roll—the dry, crusty flakes clung to the roof of my mouth. Resisting the urge to cough and sputter, I took draught of water.

"I wish I had a last name that people could pronounce and spell, like Brown. My name's been butchered more times than I care to count. Like today at graduation: 'Blanca Rrrrrock-it-an-sssskeee.' Sheesh, you'd think the announcers would practice a little before the actual ceremony."

Russell laughed, again. "Grass is always greener, I suppose." He paused. "So, *have* you ever traced your genealogy?"

I shook my head. "I know I'm Czech and Spanish, but that's about it. I can't name any ancestor who lived before my grandparents. How would I even go about looking into that?"

It was his turn to shrug. "I guess you could always try an online search engine, for starters."

Russell's father clinked his fork against his wine glass.

"I'd like to say a few words to the graduates," he began, broad grin displaying a row of bright white teeth.

I smiled. It felt strangely wonderful to sit among a group and sort of... belong. The atmosphere was so cheery, I found myself distractedly eating a little more than I knew was safe, considering that I was in a public place and needed to maintain my composure (ie. *not* puke or dissolve into fits of agony).

Sure enough, my gut didn't let my slip-up slide, as my belly-walnut steadily began to rise with a menacing gurgle. Oh, no. Not now. Anytime but now!

"And, you have worked so hard..." Russell's dad was saying.

A wave of nausea whipped my abdomen as a mighty belch escaped my lips. In an instant, every eye at the table leapt from Mr. Brown to me.

"Excuse me," I piped, unsure how on earth I managed to sound so calm. I grabbed my napkin, leapt to my feet, ran out into the blinding June light and got down on all fours behind the restaurant, by the dumpsters. Regurgitated chicken and bread dribbled from my mouth and sizzled on the hot pavement.

"Blanca!" Russell's voice called from behind.

No, no, no! My eyes scrunched shut. Why did Russell have to see me like this, *again?* I wiped my mouth in my napkin, futilely trying to block his view of the chicken-mash. "I'm fine," I choked. "Go back inside. Y-you shouldn't have to miss your grad dinner."

"It's *your* grad dinner, too." He said, dropping to his knees beside me. "And, there's no way I'm going to just leave you out here like this—" His gaze landed on my infamous golf-ball. "What's *that?*"

Instinctively, I covered the throbbing lump with the palm of my left hand. "Oh, um," I panted, "that's, uh, something that just, er... happens... after I eat. It's been going on for a couple months—since April, I think—but, my clothes are usually baggy enough to conceal—"

"A couple *months?*" Russell grunted. "Blanca, why haven't you told me? You promised to keep me updated on your symptoms!"

I was in far too much pain to tolerate a guilt-trip, right now. "Sorry," I retorted, dropping to my left side, right there on the burning tar.

* * *

So, here I am now, on July 25th, at Nation's Capital Hospital for my much-anticipated appointment with Dr. Stuart. I step through the automatic revolving door, take the elevator to the top floor and ask the lady behind the counter to check me in. She stares for a few moments like people always do when they first realize I'm albino. Then, blinking repeatedly, she asks for my name.

"Blanca Rokitansky," I say.

"Blank rocket and what?"

I shake my head. "Rokitansky. Blanca Rokitansky."

There was a long pause. The woman's cool blue eyes flicker from the screen to my face. "Hmm, well, I can't find you on today's schedule, Blanca Rocket-an-ski." Her pink nails pound the computer keyboard. "Ah, I see what happened…" Her chair scoots back. "I'm so sorry you came all the way out here, ma'am; didn't you receive a call from us, earlier this month?"

I blink. "No…"

"Well, Dr. Stuart had to cancel your appointment because he was asked to make a presentation at one of his fellowship hospitals."

"Oh." I gnaw my lip. "Well, what am I supposed to do?"

She leans forward, mouse clicking. "We have a space at 1PM on August 25th. Does that work?"

I swallow, and a pocket of air shoots down my esophagus like a bullet. "August?" I breathe hollowly. "Don't you have anything sooner?"

She slowly unwraps a stick of peppermint gum. "No, ma'am."

Sweat beads break out on my forehead, though the hospital is colder than a Canadian Christmas. "But, I-I'm about to start college, and I'm really sick."

"Being sick doesn't make you special here, sweetie," she said, gnawing her gum, voice like sour honey. "This is a hospital."

RUSSELL BROWN

A bag of corn chips and a can of cherry-cola sit before me on the kitchen table, but I can't really bring myself to open either. I wish that I could magically infuse the caloric content of both into Blanca's bloodstream. She used to be thin in a good way—like a runner, lithe and light—but, by now, she bridged the gap from slender to emaciated. On graduation day, a month ago, she looked like she might drown in her gown. No matter what, I can't erase the memory of her fragile wine-glass neck protruding from the sea of deep-blue robes, her silky white hair draped around her rosy face and delicate jaw. From their cavernous sockets stared a pair of liquid-crystal eyes, like sparkling pink lemonade, when not concealed behind those cool, reflective shades…

I return the chips to the cupboard and the soda to the fridge. Guess I lost my appetite, too.

BLANCA ROKITANSKY

November 20, 2009.

I don't have a scale here at college, but back on August 25th, when I finally went in for my first appointment at Nation's Capital, I was greeted by a big digital '77'. Gaping, the nurse kept pushing the reset button, but it was no malfunction; the horrid number just flashed over and over until the nurse finally gave in and recorded it on my chart.

I never did get to see Dr. Stuart, that day. Instead, I met with one of his interns, Dr. Gouda. Yes, spelled just like the cheese.

"Where's Dr. Stuart?" I asked after a quarter-hour of repeating my symptoms to Dr. Gouda's blank face.

"He's a very busy person," the pimply man-boy replied.

"That's exactly why I waited 4 months for this appointment," I sighed.

All I managed to glean from Dr. Teenage Face that afternoon was an explanation of the Body Mass Index Scale: above 25 is overweight, 20-24 is healthy, under 18.5 is underweight and under 15 indicates danger of organ failure and cardiac arrest. At 5'5" and 77 pounds, my BMI that day was 12.5. His recommendation?

"Gain some weight, and fast."

"But, how am I supposed to do that when eating hurts?"

He didn't answer. "Sorry, but your time is up, and Dr. Stuart really hates it when I get off-schedule. We'll talk about it at a future appointment, okay? Go have some burgers and ice cream; that's my prescription." With that, he handed me a sheet of general information on Irritable Bowel Syndrome printed from the internet and a note recommending some painkillers and over-the-counter gas meds.

Summer break ended the following day. Moving into my dorm, my suitemates stared openly and whispered behind their hands. Only one girl had the nerve to actually ask me to my face if I was anorexic. It wasn't long before I started withdrawing from my peers and spending most of my time just with Russell.

After only a couple weeks into the semester, I became so weak, the physical aspect of college life was almost impossible. I lived in a dorm that was a 45-minute walk from central campus and more than 12 flights of stairs up from the street, with no elevators. I couldn't go anywhere without taking rests on the curb. I stopped bringing half the required books to class because I couldn't lift them. I grew faint and dizzy when sitting in lecture. I was always so cold, I wore leggings under my pants and turtlenecks under my sweaters. Sometimes, I wore a winter coat and gloves indoors. I skipped half my extracurriculars out of exhaustion. Every night, I had tremors and palpitations that made it difficult to breathe and impossible to fall asleep.

But, worst of all was the stabbing in my stomach. Often, I'd have to lie face-down after a meal from pain, even if that meant stretching out on the chairs in the dining halls. Food caused so much agony that, on exam days, I refused to eat at all, so I could concentrate a little better.

One September day, I tried to jog after a bus that was about to leave without me, and debilitating pain struck me in the center of my chest—I'd never felt anything like it before. I stumbled to the ground, dropping my backpack, hands numb, chest heaving, unable to breathe. The bus stopped and the next thing I knew, someone onboard had called for an ambulance. At the hospital, I was given an EKG and a consultation with a rather harried-looking doctor.

"Your heart is a muscle," he explained, hastily. "And, just as you've lost so much muscle from the rest of your body, you probably lost some of your heart muscle too, because you're so underweight. So, now, your heart has to work very hard—pumping very fast—to supply enough blood and oxygen."

I mentioned my continual stomach pain, and he told me what I've heard many times before: that I probably had Irritable Bowel Syndrome. IBS was common and incurable. Once more, I faced myself with the prospect of feeling like this every day for the rest of my life. The idea was unbearable.

I was convinced that it had to be something more serious. Something treatable.

* * *

September passed in a flurry of intensive medical exams. The tests were grueling, some even barbaric. I was scanned, biopsied, scoped, prodded, poked, injected, infused, dehydrated, starved, strapped to a tilt-table and turned upside-down, fed literal liters of radioactive chemicals, and even landed in the ER twice from allergic reactions to the IV and oral fluids. The Department of Bowel Diseases determined by the end of the month that there was nothing physical causing my symptoms.

"We've ruled out all the basic stomach and colon stuff," Dr. Pimpleface told me on September 30th. "No H. Pylori, Celiac Disease, food allergies, stomach ulcers, colon polyps, colitis, cancers nor pelvic dysfunctions. If it's not Irritable Bowel Syndrome, it's anorexia nervosa."

"I'm not anorexic; I'm in *pain*," I whimpered for the umpteenth time that fall, "serious pain."

"It's probably all in your head. How about I write you a referral for our eating disorder clinic?"

The moment I exited the hospital, I ripped that referral into tiny shreds. Then, I called Russell to give him the verdict.

He breathed loudly into the receiver. "Your doctors aren't thinking *rare,* and they're focusing exclusively on your stomach and colon and forgetting everything in-between. They're testing you for the same old stuff that you were checked for when you were 8 because it's routine and easy. They need to hunt for things that *aren't* common. Zebras, not horses."

"Well, my case has just been dismissed by the Department of Bowel Diseases," I wailed. "Dr. Gouda pawned me off to the eating disorder clinic. Can I come over and do my homework in your room tonight?" I was too miserable to spend the evening alone.

"Of course."

The hours passed slowly and torturously, that evening. I sat on Russell's bed with my laptop and textbooks, unable to focus on the essay on the American judicial system that I was supposed to be writing. It was due the following week, on October 5th. Giving up, I minimized my world processor and opened my internet browser.

Scanning my email inbox, I began mindlessly deleting notifications from the social networking site I'd reluctantly joined at the beginning of the semester. I rolled my eyes when I saw that my own mom had sent me a 'friend request.' So much for these sites being for students only. I wonder who'll 'friend' me next, my grandparents?

Grandparents. Hmm. Remembering what Russell had said about researching genealogy, I spontaneously typed my own last name into a search engine and hit enter. Almost all the results on the first page were about a 'Baron Carl Von Rokitansky.' I clicked the top link, Quickipedia Encyclopedia:

'Born on February 19, 1804, Baron Carl Von Rokitansky was a Bohemian physician, pathologist, philosopher and politician. He is renowned for developing the 'in-situ' method of autopsy, which is no longer in use today. Rokitansky is said to have supervised 70,000 autopsies over the course of 45 years, personally performing over 30,000 at an average of 2 a day, 7 days a week.'

My nose wrinkled. The article listed a handful of diseases and disorders that Rokitansky discovered, the first of which was, '*Superior Mesenteric Artery (SMA) Syndrome, a gastro-vascular disorder whose existence as a distinct clinical entity remains controversial until today.*'

"How can a disease's *existence* be controversial?" I wondered aloud, forgetting that I wasn't alone in the room.

"What did you say, Blanca?" Russell hummed, eyes still fixated on his own computer.

"Nothing, just talking to myself."

"'Bout what?"

"Oh, I'm just randomly reading about some Bohemian medical doctor from the 1800s who has my last name." My hand waved.

"Bohemia, huh? That's where the Czech Republic is today. How cool would it be if he were your actual ancestor?"

I froze.

"So, what's the guy famous for?" Russell pressed on.

"Cutting open a lot of dead people and discovering the rare diseases that killed them."

At this, Russell swiveled in his seat. "Which diseases?"

I shrugged. "What does it matter?"

Abandoning his desk, he scooted beside me on the bed and began perusing the article over my shoulder.

"Select the first one," he said, "Superior Mesenteric Artery Syndrome."

I obeyed, and the screen promptly displayed: '*This article does not exist. Want to create it? Click here.*'

"Will you look at that," Russell breathed. "I thought Quickipedia covered everything. Well, just plug it into a search engine, then."

I followed suit. A very short list of results came up, each resource with no more than 3-4 lines on the condition, apiece.

"Only 500 cases have been recorded in English-language medical literature since the condition's discovery in 1861," Russell read with fascination. "Wow, now, that's *rarer* than rare!"

I was starting to get annoyed. Who cared? This had nothing to do with anything.

"Russell, I know you find this sort of thing fascinating and all," I sighed, "but I don't."

"Hold on a sec." He leaned in. "Symptoms include early satiety, nausea, projectile vomiting, upper-left-flank abdominal pain, abdominal distention, eructation and severe malnutrition," he read. "Patients with the chronic, congenital form of SMA syndrome predominantly have a lengthy or even life-long history of abdominal complaints with intermittent exacerbations depending on the degree of duodenal compression. As the syndrome involves a lack of essential fat, 90% of the afflicted are underweight, often to the point of emaciation. Females are impacted twice as often as males, with 75% of cases occurring between the ages of 10 and 30."

Wait, what?

"It's a condition that only happens to thin people," Russell paraphrased the next paragraph, "and it makes them even thinner. Major 'attacks' can be set off in a predisposed person by anything that kicks off the weight-loss spiral, even by just a few pounds." He looked at me. "Like your flu this past spring."

"Now, *you* hold on a second." I snapped the laptop shut. "We can't just start suspecting that I have some random rare disease that we stumbled upon on the internet. That's crazy."

"Blanca, this description fits your case *perfectly*. And, like I said earlier, I think the *reason* your doctors have been unsuccessful thus far is because they *aren't* considering the rare stuff. Like SMA Syndrome."

I hated how much sense he was making.

"It can't hurt to ask a gastroenterologist about it and let him order you a CT to rule it out," he suggested, "right?"

Wrong. I went ahead and scheduled an appointment with Dr. Benjamin Stuart—insisting this time that I see the man himself rather than any of his interns. After months of waiting, I went in yesterday, Wednesday, November 18th. The old man literally laughed in my face at the mere mention of SMA Syndrome.

"That so-called 'disorder' isn't real," he said flatly, about 30 seconds into my appointment. "It's smokescreen for the eating-disordered. Speaking of which, have you followed my intern's orders to start therapy at our ED clinic?"

I was dismissed from the appointment about 15 seconds after that. Trudging back to my dorm in defeat, I called Russell to tell him what went down.

"So, I'm guessing he didn't order you the CT."

"Nope. Said I didn't need it and that it'd be a waste of hospital resources and technician hours."

"Yeah, that sounds like The Stool, alright."

"Do you think any other GI would write me the order?"

"No way. Dr. Suart is their boss and no one—I mean, *no one*—double-crosses him."

"Then, what should we do? Start my case over at a new hospital?"

"That'd take too long. You need to have that scan, like, yesterday."

"How?"

There was a pause. "I think I have an idea. What are you doing tomorrow evening?"

RUSSELL BROWN

Friday, November 20th, 8:01PM.

I don't have my technician certification yet. I'm still in training—definitely not authorized to administer a computed tomography scan on my own. I have the keys to a mobile CT, but only because it's part of my orderly duties to move and park it at the discretion of the docs and techs.

Swallowing, I exit the building, trying to look as calm and normal as possible as I walk briskly across the parking lot. A group of young men in scrubs, smoking while leaning against a dormant ambulance, nod at me as I approach. It always perplexes me, to see *medical* staff *smoking*. Especially while so close to the intake vent of a building full of sick people. For heaven's sake.

Anyway, I just nod back stiffly, avoiding eye-contact. Great. A crowd of witnesses is just what I need. But, it's too late to turn around, now—it's already obvious to any onlooker where I'm headed. So, I have to act like I'm *supposed* to be doing what I'm doing; turning back would just seem suspicious.

"Where are you taking the scanner, Russ? Aren't you done for the day, by now?" a voice calls the second I jam my key into the door of the vehicle. It's Mark, the lead tech. Wonderful.

"Nope, not yet," I answer, voice just a *little* too high. I did indeed clock out at 8PM. I make a mental note to swipe the posted orderly schedule from above the fax machine, the following morning.

"A little late for break, isn't it?"

"Oh, I'm not on break," I say, oh-so-casually. "Joel asked me to bring the mobile CT out back."

"What for? There aren't anymore outpatient scans scheduled for today."

"I dunno what's going on," I babble. "Probably for an ER patient or something."

At those words, one of the smokers—a man with 'EMS' stamped on his shoulder—perks up.

"Or, maybe, its for an inpatient," I say quickly. "I've just been asked to park it out back, so that's what I'm going to do." I swallow. "I should go, now."

And, before Mark or anyone else could ask more questions, I yank the door open, scramble onboard and peel off. I leave the hospital campus entirely, heading for an out-of-service gas station, a few miles away. I park by a dumpster behind an abandoned convenience store, arriving just in time to see Blanca hopping off the city bus, a couple blocks away. She approaches with her head down and her hands in her pockets, body a little white spec in the dark night. Small clouds of condensation puff from her bluish lips and into the frigid air.

I unlock the backdoor so she can let herself in. I pull a heavy lead vest over my chest, lean over the control panel, and flick a switch in the center. The CT behind me whirrs to life.

The back pops open and I hear Blanca grunt faintly as she hoists herself up.

"Hey," she greets me, breathlessly.

"Hey," I answer, voice as weak as hers— though, unlike her, I didn't just emerge from a hike in the cold while vastly underweight. I'm just scared to death. I never stuck a live person with a needle before, only cadavers. I wish I could wait until I'm fully trained before attempting it on my best friend, but being as Blanca's life is literally wasting away before our very eyes, there isn't exactly time. At the rate she's deteriorating, she could be dead before I get my technician certification.

Blanca's pink eyes, violet in the dark-blue light filtering through the windshield, settle on the tube.

"I can't believe we're doing this," she murmurs. "I can't believe we stole a CT scanner."

My pulse quickens all the more. "We didn't *steal* it," I reply, pulling on a pair of purple rubber gloves that are much too small. "We're borrowing it."

I attach a bag of intravenous contrast agent to a stand and take a .22 needle in hand. Such a big needle. I stare at its massive silver tip, glinting in the flickering florescent light. The standard for adults is .18. And, Blanca's veins are so delicate, she usually requires a pediatric 'butterfly' needle. But, CT IVs require no less than .22 so the solution can flow at the proper rate.

Blanca unzips her jacket, rosy eyes expressionless.

"Ready?" I ask, giving her what I hope is a reassuring smile as I run through the steps in my head. Barium first, IV second. Then, 10-15 minutes to let the solution exit her belly and enter her duodenum. Then, take 10 pictures separated by 2 minutes each. "Nothing to eat or drink for at least 8 hours? Not wearing any metal?"

"Yes, sir."

"Alight, then. Your barium is on the counter. Shake it well and drink the whole thing. You'll be in the tube in 10."

She nods, looking even paler than usual, if that's possible. I watch from the corner of my vision as she swirls the bottle about and pops it open.

She begins to sip in silence, face already twisted from the pain of a few ounces entering her stomach. Blood churning in my ears, I adjust the scanner settings, retrieve a couple bandages from an overhead cabinet and prep the alcohol swab. I try very hard not to think about what I'm about to do and who I'm doing it to. Blanca is the last person I'd want to hurt. Heaven knows she's already had enough pain for a dozen lifetimes.

BLANCA ROKITANSKY

I lie on the narrow bench, Russell kneeling to my right, close enough for me to see the sweat droplets forming at his curly hairline, even without my glasses.

"Nervous?" I whisper.

He smiles, wanly. "I just have a little tummy ache, that's all."

"Aw, I'm sorry." I touch his shoulder.

"No, *I'm* sorry," he chortles. "I know I really shouldn't complain about belly pain to *you*, of all people."

"Don't apologize." I frown. "My pain doesn't disqualify or diminish yours in any way. It doesn't work like that."

He shrugs. "I suppose."

"I'm really sorry about this whole thing," I add. "This must be so scary for you."

His brows scrunch. "For *me?* I'm not the one about to get stuck with a giant needle by an 18-year-old orderly." His voice cracks a little.

"I didn't mean to put you under this kind of pressure and make you risk your job and everything," I babble. "I know how much you love your job, and how this could mess up your chances of getting into medical school if we're caught—"

"Medical school?" His corkscrewed hair bounces with the abrupt turn of his head. "My job? You think I'm worried about those things, *now?*" He sleeve-wipes his face. "Blanca, you're dyi—um, really, really ill." He swallows. "If I save your life but get banned from every med school in the nation, then so be it."

He then takes my pencil-like arm into his purple-gloved hands, ties the tourniquet tightly just below my shoulder, and begins feeling for a vein. For once, my pallor is useful for something—the blue lines, thin as they are, are perfectly visible.

"Your veins are *so* tiny," he murmurs, warm fingers running up and down my forearm. "This needle could probably tear one right open and you'd hemorrhage out—"

Horrified, I pull away.

Russell's tan cheeks adopt a slight rosy twinge. "I-I'm so sorry—just thinking aloud—

stupid thing to say—didn't mean a word of it," he sputters, "please, ignore me—y-you're going to be fine. Everything's going to be fine."

"Who exactly are you reassuring?" I ask, weakly.

He doesn't answer.

"I think I found one," he says excitedly, a minute or so later. He tears open a rubbing-alcohol packet with urgency, as though afraid to lose the vein if an extra millisecond passes. He swabs me, drops the towelette on the floor, then snatches up the massive needle.

"On the count of 3." He inhales. "1… 2…"

I close my eyes and wait for the sting. A long pause ensues.

"I-I think I'll count backward from 5 instead, okay?" he chokes.

"Um, sure. Whatever makes you comfortable."

"Alright, then." He exhales. "5… 4… 3… 2…"

My eyes flutter shut.

Another long silence.

"I don't know how surgeons do it, really," comes Russell's voice.

My lids crack open.

"I mean, a *needle* is scary enough. How on earth do they cut people open with those *huge* scalpels? Maybe, it's easier because the patient has been put under…?" His eyes grow to yellow traffic lights.

"So, put me under," I suggest, though I was downright terrified by the idea of being knocked unconscious by a nervous teenager holding a giant needle while hiding out in an exorbitantly-expensive stolen vehicle parked by a dumpster in an abandoned lot.

"I can't; I'd have to give you an IV for the sedative. Plus, I need you awake for the scan; you're going to have to hold your breath on cue about a dozen times."

"Oh."

His hands tremble, ever-so-slightly. "I could probably do this to a stranger, no prob. But, not my best friend."

Best friend? My stomach jumps, though heavy with a cupful of barium. Russell has a lot of friends—a lot of 'cool' friends, like the guys on the basketball team. Did he really consider *me* his number one?

"They cover the faces of the cadavers you practice on, right?" I ask, thinking back to a cheesy med-school drama I recently watched.

He nods. "Makes things seem less real, less personal. Like I'm sticking a pillow instead of a person."

"Well, how about we cover *my* face, then? Throw on a towel, or something."

He blinks. "You'd be okay with that?"

"Of course. Anything to make this easier for you… as long as I don't suffocate," I add, only half-joking.

"A-alright then." He puts the needle down (whew) and walks around the tube. I hear a drawer squeak and the next thing I know, a sterile-smelling white cloth is draped over my head.

"On the count of 3," Russell declares, once more. "1… 2… 3."

I feel the needle pierce my flesh, swiftly and cleanly.

"YEAH!" he shouts, startling me so badly, I fight the impulse to jump up and wrench the precious IV right back out. "YEAH, I did it!" he hoots again, taping the needle down.

"Great job," I say as I bat the towel away. He releases the tourniquet and warm blood rushes back into my fingertips. Then, he gets to his feet and flicks a switch on the

IV line, allowing the contrast agent to begin its course.

"It's flowing at the slowest possible rate," he says, all excitement abruptly vanquished from his voice. "But, even *that* is probably far faster than your own blood-flow."

"What does that mean?"

"Well… um… it means that this may feel a bit… intense."

He pushes a few buttons on the control panel and the machine groans as the bench slides inside the funnel of dancing lights.

"Intense?" I squeak.

"Just don't freak out, okay? Side-effects are normal. Try to hold still or you'll ruin the pictures."

"What kind of side-effects are we talking about?"

Almost instantly, I feel a hot wave of invisible lava sweep over my entire body.

"Oh!" I look down my needled arm and see veins protruding all the way to my shoulder like black spider-webs.

Alarmed, I try to say something, but my voice gets caught in my throat as it tightens. Blood churns in my ears as my head pounds. I press my tongue down in my jaw and tilt my head back, desperate to open my airways. My saliva, metallic like water from a rusted drinking-fountain, rolls back into my throat, gagging me. My bladder contracts involuntarily. I strongly wish I'd thought of using the restroom beforehand. Just what I need to do—pee my pants in front of Russell. First puking, and now this. Am I going to have *any* dignity left by the time this whole medical masquerade is over?

"Everything alright in there?" Russell's voice sounds on the intercom.

"Y-yes," I choke through swollen lymph nodes.

Just when I thought things couldn't get any worse, my hands and feet begin to prickle.

"A-am I s-supposed to go n-numb?" I whimper, teeth chattering despite the hot-flashes. "I c-can't feel m-my arms or l-legs."

"It's perfectly normal; don't worry." His voice is high. Strange what qualifies as 'normal' in the world of health science. "Hold your breath," he orders. Not like I can breathe all that well, anyway.

I suck in whatever air I can manage and bite down on my tongue. Just don't pee, Blanca. Whatever you do, don't wet yourself.

"Okay, breathe!"

I gulp at the air, open-mouthed.

The order comes again, "Hold your breath!"

As I close my lips, the metallic flavor intensifies, like I'm sucking on a dirty quarter.

"Breathe!"

The pattern continues for what seems like hours, until the much-anticipated words arrive: "We're done. Let's get you out of there."

Russell slaps a button and emerges from behind the screen while I slide from the tube. He rips off the tape holding down the needle—along with a few white armhairs—and pulls out the IV. Almost instantly, the symptoms begin to subside. Everything except the blaring headache.

He presses a cotton ball against the puncture and tapes it so tightly, my arm feels as though submerged in a blowfish tank.

"You okay?" he asks.

I nod, breathing heavily, clothes damp with cold sweat. Russell hands me my glasses and when I put them on, I see that his chest is trembling beneath the heavy vest and his hair is one giant, rumpled, curly knot.

"You did it," I breathe. "You ran a scan, all by yourself. You're a tech!"

His tired face dimples with a grin. "Not *all* by myself. I doubt my future patients will offer to let me smother them with a towel."

I laugh.

He stands. "The computer is burning a CD of your images, now." He sheds the vest. "We have what we need. Now, let's get this half-million-dollar truck back to the hospital before someone notices I'm taking *way* too long to park it out back."

RUSSELL BROWN

I'm no doctor, but what I see now is undeniable. I lean in, peering anxiously at the computer screen, at the greyscale images of the cross-section of Blanca's abdomen. It doesn't take a radiologist to see that she has a serious bowel obstruction, whether induced by the superior mesenteric artery or not. Blanca's duodenum isn't a tube, but a *funnel*—an enormous white balloon that abruptly narrows into blackness. It's so obvious that I can't help but wonder why this wasn't caught before; Blanca said she was x-rayed back when she first started exhibiting symptoms at age 8. If she does indeed have the chronic, congenital form of SMA Syndrome, then *something* should've shown up back then. A distention like this can't develop overnight; this has to be the product of years and years of pressure.

I sneak a peak to the left and right. The lobby of the Department of Bowel Diseases is quiet. Jim and Colin are on break, and all the doctors seem to be caught up in their streams of appointments. My only company is a handful of patients in the waiting room. Biting my lip, I click on the digital directory of patient records. Name? *Blanca Rokitansky.* Birthdate? *06/21/1989.*

A rather extensive list of hospitalizations appears. Eyes sliding down the page, I select *CT with PO Contrast, Abdomen & Pelvis - 07/07/1997* and expand the tab. *Impression: Normal CT,* the conclusion of the report reads, electronically signed by none other than a dozen-year-younger Dr. Benjamin Stuart. Huh. I had no idea he used to practice radiology. Perplexed, I open the image file. And, sure enough, at first glance, Blanca's pictures seem like nothing special. Squinting, I bring my face within a couple inches of the screen. Blanca's tininess sure makes the awkward-cross-section very compact and difficult to discern. I click the magnifying-glass icon on the toolbar, draw a box around the second and third portions of her duodenum and zoom in as far as I can.

And, that's when I see it. The funnel. Oh, yes, it's minor. Perhaps a little *too* minor to catch the eye of someone who isn't specifically hunting for this rare disease. But, it's definitely there. It'd probably be far more apparent on a face-front Upper GI Series. But, of course, no one thought to order a UGI after the CT was stamped 'normal.' UGIs, which are far more time-consuming and expensive, are typically reserved for confirming initial diagnoses made from suspicious CTs.

The constriction and dilation were fairly mild. No doubt, if caught and treated back then, Blanca wouldn't be dying today. Back then, she probably could've gotten by with a couple weeks on a feeding tube, so the mesenteric fat pad could grow large enough to relieve the constriction. Now, however, it looks like she'll have to undergo major surgery.

"You alright there, Russell?" Colin's voice sounds from the doorway. He and Jim are back from break. I quickly minimize the patient database.

"Yeah, sure, of course," I say, tone an octave too high. "Why wouldn't I be?"

A red brow creeps up Colin's pink forehead. "You were staring knives at that computer screen."

"Oh, was I?" I shrug, oh-so-casually ejecting Blanca's CD.

"Russell Brown?" a sharp voice calls from the doorway.

I turn. It's Mark, holding a copy of the orderly schedule. My sweaty hands tremble on the disk.

"Yes, sir?"

"I need to talk to you, now. Privately, please."

Without a word, I follow him out, incriminating evidence literally in hand. This is it. Mark knows. He saw me leave in the mobile CT last night, and he knows now that I was off the clock. My heart sinks to the floor. I didn't even have time to get Blanca's images to a doctor!

Mark takes me to the radiology backroom, where doctors usually sit in the semi-darkness to review streams of milky-white scans. The office is empty now because it's after 5PM. I tail him to a desk in the back-left corner, flanked by a couple oversized computer screens.

"Sit," he orders.

Nervously, I perch in the seat beside him.

"Okay, I'm just going to cut to the chase, here," he says, tone icy. "I want to know what the hell you were up to, yesterday evening. I ran into Joel at lunch today and chided him about making his orderlies work late, and he said he doesn't know what on earth I'm talking about. He said you were out the door by 8PM, as scheduled." He rattles the sheet. "So, apparently, he never asked you to park the mobile CT out back." His arms fold. "And, first thing this morning, when I took a patient onboard, I noticed a few supplies were missing and saw an empty IV bag and needle in the bio-waste bin. Usually, units are restocked at the end of each day, and the trash is taken out."

I swallow. Shoot, why didn't I think to remove the garbage bag? How was I so negligent!?

"I don't know what the hell you think you're doing, running off in a half-million dollar scanner and stealing hospital equipment. You're the absolute last person I'd expect something like this from—a *Presidential Scholar* with a free ride to *medical school?*

You better have a damn good reason to risk all that."

I look down at the CD in my damp hands. The truth is wilder than any fiction he could possibly dream up, right?

"Were you using our needles and equipment to do drugs?" he snaps. "Meeting up with other junkies in the truck?"

What? "No," I breathe. So, a black teenager is being accused of sneaking off to do drugs. Shocker. "That's not it, at all."

"Then, what were you doing in there, Russell? I'm waiting."

Here goes nothing. Wordlessly, I pop the disk into the computer's drive.

"My best friend is sick," I begin, loading the first image. "I mean, really, *really* sick. She's dying, wasting away at age 18, but no one is taking her seriously. Dr. Stuart insists that she has an eating disorder, but I know that isn't it. There's something seriously wrong with her GI tract. Something physical preventing her from digesting food. No doctor has been willing to prescribe the tests she needs, because they're convinced her problem is psychological. So, last night, I…"

Speechless, his lips part.

"I know what I did was wrong," I continue. "I'm willing to pay out-of-pocket for the cost of the scan, go to jail, get fired, lose my scholarship, whatever. If it saves her life…"

Mark blinks, mouth still agape. "You ran a contrast-CT on a patient last night, by yourself?" he asks, faintly.

I nod.

"And, your friend—she's okay? No hemorrhaging or other side-effects?"

"Nothing out of the ordinary."

He peers back at the screen, eyes like traffic-lights. "Your friend *is* sick," he breathes. "I'm no doctor, but I can usually tell if a scan is normal or not. Her bowels are horribly misshapen."

I swallow. "We think she may have a rare gastro-vascular disorder called Superior Mesenteric Artery Syndrome."

He pauses for a moment, brows scrunching together like furry centipedes. "Who's 'we'? I thought you said all her doctors are convinced its anorexia."

"They are…"

His gaze narrows. "So, this is the speculation of a pair of 18-year-old college freshmen?"

"I know it sounds a little crazy, but—"

"It's more than a *little crazy*, Russell; it's downright foolish, to even *try* hypothesizing." He throws his hands up. "You're a couple of *kids*, for crying out loud. You're bright, I'll give you that, but don't get a big head and start thinking you're now a physician just because you can stick an IV." He ejects the CD and, to my astonishment, hands it back to me. "I've never heard of this super arterial disease, anyway—"

"Superior Mesenteric Artery Syndrome," I snap.

"Whatever. I don't know where you dug that up, but you better think twice before throwing the names of rare, frightening diseases in your sick friend's gullible face. If she's willing to let you stick her with a needle and pump a bag of chemicals into her veins, then she must be very desperate or naïve or both. Don't abuse people's trust."

"That wasn't my intention, sir. I really did—do—think we have sufficient reason to believe that she has SMA Syndrome. She's been sick her whole life, so just about everything has been ruled out by now *except* the really rare stuff. We just needed this test to see if—"

"I've sorted through thousands of radiology reports in my lifetime and I've never seen a *single* mention of that condition. Not *one*."

"Well, only about 500 cases have been reported in all of *history*, so..."

"Russell!"

"I know, I know." I shove the CD into the pocket of my scrubs. "But, I still think it's worth investigating. You're the head tech; maybe, you could give the disk to one of the radiologists and ask—"

"And, ask them what, Russell?" he cuts me off. "You want me to give my superiors an unmarked, unregistered CD and say that an orderly ran off with my scanner to test his dying best friend because no doctor was willing?"

I stay silent.

"I can't tell them the truth, and you can't ask me to lie for you. Do you want to get me fired? Forget fired—do you want to get me arrested?" He logs off the computer and gets to his feet. "What you did was crazy, irresponsible, dangerous and illegal. But, I don't think you deserve to lose your future over it. Heaven knows the world needs more medical professionals willing to go out on a limb for their patients, like you have. So, I'm not going to report the theft, and you can keep your CD. But, that's it. I'm not doing a damn thing more for you. Believe me, I'm letting you off easy." He stands. "From now on, if you nick so much as a paperclip, you'll be out of here like *this*." His fingers snap. "Understood?"

"Yes, sir."

He holds out his hand. "Keys, please?"

I hand over my copy of the mobile CT keys.

"A word of advice," he breezes on. "If you value your reputation, at all—if you want to be taken seriously as a future doctor—drop the rare disease babble, now. You need some serious credentials before you start tossing around wild claims like that. If you find a radiologist willing to look at that CD without reporting you to the authorities, don't mention a word about some crazy syndrome. Let the doctors reach their own conclusions." He zips his coat. "Oh, and by the way, I'd like to schedule your tech certification exam a few months early. How does a couple weeks from tomorrow sound?"

RUSSELL BROWN

The first day of Thanksgiving break.

Blanca sits across from me at her mom's kitchen table, delicate jaw literally dropping. I just told her what went down with Mark, yesterday—how he found out about our adventure with the mobile scanner, let me off the hook, then refused to pass her scans to a radiologist.

"Basically, he'd rather let you die than risk getting fired," I conclude.

"Well, he's right," she says, to my surprise.

I plunk down my can of cherry-cola. "Right about what?"

"About this… rare disease stuff." She wrings her hands. "Russell, you could lose everything by pushing the whole SMA Syndrome thing. We got away with the scan, but you can't get away with a controversial diagnosis that even the most esteemed doctors are hesitant to advocate. You're an orderly. Keep talking like this and no one's going to take you seriously when you apply for medical school—they'll think you're crazy or something."

"Blanca, how are you not getting this, by now?" I explode. "Do you think I *care* about my stupid reputation when you're *dying?*"

At once, her cheeks grow as pink as her irises.

"Oh, my goodness, I-I'm so sorry," I sputter, "Blanca, I didn't mean to…" I touch the back of her hand.

"It's not you," she grunts, holding her stomach, "I-I think that juice I just drank isn't… agreeing with me."

She sprints to the sink. Face in the drain, her entire frame shakes violently. Orange juice pours from her lips and down her ivory chin. After several minutes of heaving, she peers up at me, eyes hollow and bloodshot, body still trembling, strings of mucus dangling from her lips.

"Russell," she whispers, "a-am I really going to die?"

I swallow. SMA Syndrome has a mortality rate of 1:3. Blanca was, what, now, 70 pounds? 65? I close my eyes and take a deep breath, about to give the first of many bad-news-deliveries that darkens the life of a medical professional:

"I… don't know. Maybe."

RUSSELL BROWN

"You know how patients scare themselves, looking up rare diseases on the internet and deluding themselves into thinking that they're going to die?" Dr. Stuart says to no one in particular, leaning against the front desk behind which Jim, Colin and I are sitting. The Stool just came out of an appointment. Pretending to ignore him, I continue plugging in a list of patient addresses and phone numbers into our database. "They psyche themselves up and run into my office at top speed, convinced they're going to collapse any minute because they can pick out a couple symptoms listed on the web under some horrid, fatal disease." His head shakes vigorously, copious belly jiggling. "I mean, I have a patient convinced she has Superior Mesenteric Artery Syndrome. *Really.*" My heart skips a beat as my typing rhythm breaks. He looks down at Colin. "Can you believe that?"

"Never heard of it," Colin answers, passively.

"That's because it doesn't exist."

Colin smirks. "Then, where'd she dig up the name? A movie or something?"

"Its existence as a pathological clinical entity is controversial," I interject, voice low, "but, it *has* been described in valid medical literature."

Dr. Stuart's gaze meets mine. "Been doing some doomsday research yourself, huh?"

"Yeah, it's a macabre hobby of mine," I find myself saying, "reading about medicine. I guess it has something to do with wanting to become a doctor, one day—you know, saving the lives of people even if their diseases *aren't* easy to diagnose or treat."

Dr. Stuart's face instantly transforms from bemused to furious.

"For your information, SMA Syndrome isn't 'medicine,'" he barks. "It isn't a real condition; it's a hokey theory—a smokescreen for eating-disorder patients who don't want to own up to the *real* reason they're starving to death."

"Maybe, if we stopped assuming patients are mentally ill and actually run some tests—"

"Then, we'll find that symptoms don't always correlate with radiologic findings, and may not even improve after major intestinal bypass surgery," he cuts across me, reciting an argument championed by the unfortunately-influential Dr. B. Shandling in an article published almost 40 years ago. Yes, 40. That's the problem with ancients like Dr. Stuart.

"Maybe, the bypass doesn't necessarily cure all the symptoms immediately because the enteric nervous system can be totally rewired by the disease and the memory patterns aren't instantly forgotten after surgery," I echoed a Chinese study published in the *World Journal of Gastroenterology* just under 2 years ago. "With SMA Syndrome, the intestines learn to pump backward, and it can keep it up for a while even after the original impetus—the blockage—has been relieved."

"Reversed peristalsis," he names the phenomenon I described. "It would take a *substantial* physical obstruction for a *prolonged* period of time for the enteric nervous system to override a *lifetime* of programming. Direct peristalsis is hardwired memory."

"Not if the patient has SMA Syndrome their whole life. In that case, reversed peristalsis would be the norm, wouldn't it?"

Dr. Stuart breathed out. "These are wild hypotheses you are making."

"Who said *I* made them?"

"In all of history, there've been less than 500 descriptions of people with vaguely-similar symptoms and radiologic findings. That's not enough to prove a damn thing. If that's all it takes to coin a new disease, then we'd have a disease for everything. Colin just dropped his pencil now because he has Pencil Dropping Syndrome."

Colin puts his hands up. "Hey, keep me out of this."

"How obscure can a *mechanical obstruction* really be?" I grumble. "It can be seen. Back in the 1800s, it was first described in patients at *autopsy*. It killed them."

"Are you saying it's more likely that an *18-year-old college girl* is too thin because of an extremely rare, life-threatening syndrome rather than an eating disorder?"

"No, I'm not saying it's more *likely*. But, the right diagnosis isn't always the most obvious!"

At that moment, Dr. Stuart's pager beeps. With one last scathing glare, he takes off.

"You're crazy," Colin informs me at the very same moment Jim breathes, "You're a freaking prodigy!"

There's an awkward silence.

"No, he's crazy," Colin insists. "No one—and, I mean, *no one*—argues medicine with a nationwide top-10 doc. I can't believe Dr. Stuart even bothered to talk back, Russ. You're an *orderly*."

"He's technically a tech, now. Got his cert yesterday," Jim comments.

"Something I said must've struck a chord, if he got so upset," I murmur, frustrated beyond belief. How could anyone, let alone a prestigious doctor, look poor Blanca in the eye and deny that her pain is real?

BLANCA ROKITANSKY

Fall slowly crystallizes into winter. Now, I'm only a handful of final-exams away from Christmas break.

A couple weeks ago, Dr. Stuart put me on a pediatric nasogastric tube. "Because you won't eat enough by mouth," he said.

"Not *won't*," I insisted. "*Can't.*"

Bringing the tube to class is downright mortifying. Every day, people stare openly at the anorexic-looking albino girl with a plastic pipe protruding from her left nostril, hooked to a 5-foot metal stand bearing a bag of off-white goo. I have to stay hooked to the thing at least 20 hours a day because my body cannot tolerate anything but the slowest pumping speed. As a result, I'm not gaining any weight. I'm barely maintaining at 65 pounds.

I have nightmares on a regular basis; I dream that I'm disappearing, like a ghost in the wind. Most mornings, I awake to the machinelike noises of my NG tube, surprised to find that I'm still alive.

Russell and I study together each evening. He always comes to my dorm so I won't have to make the embarrassingly-short-but-exhausting one-hundred-yard trek to his. These days, I only go out to attend my classes. No more literature club or debate team or honor society. I don't have the energy for them.

Sometimes, after we're done with our homework, we just sit on the suite couch in front of my roommate's television, fear of the future silently filling the room and rendering us unable to even chuckle at the characters' silly sitcom lives. Sometimes, Russell reaches out and holds my hand, eyes glazed over, completely oblivious to whatever show or movie is playing. That's my cue to start feeling guilty for having such a negative impact on his life. Before he met me, he was a normal, happy kid. But, now that he has a 'dying girl' for a best friend, it's like his spirit is trampled. He rarely cracks a smile anymore; when he *does*, it's always strained. *I'm* the one who's sick—why should others have to suffer? Russell is far too young to have to deal with any of this.

Watching him now, hunching over a thick textbook and reciting the phases of mitosis and meiosis under his breath, I wonder for the umpteenth time what on earth made him want to become a physician in the first place. I just don't understand why anyone would engage in a rigorous 8-year program of study for a job that requires one to spend the rest of their days in a hospital full of sick, dying people.

"Russell," I suddenly blurt, "what made you want to become a doctor?"

He looks up at me, surprised.

"Sorry if that's random," I pipe.

He shrugs. "Why does anyone want to become a doctor? Why are *you* interested in English lit?"

It was my turn to shrug.

After a long draught from his soda can, he says, "I dunno, I just find the human body kind of interesting, the way you find literature interesting. I stink at writing 20-page English papers, have no special love for math or physics, and fall asleep the second someone turns on the news. So, I'm going into bio. Gotta pick something, right?"

My head shakes. "No, you didn't pick medicine by the process of elimination. No one starts working in a hospital at 17, or plans on being in school until at least 25, or turns their whole life upside-down to get involved in a random classmate's personal medical crisis... just because they find the human body 'kind of interesting.' You aren't going into medicine because you can't find anything else to do—you freaking *love* this stuff. I sometimes find your intensity frightening, to be perfectly honest," I chortle. "There must be something fueling that obsessive love. Something motivating you to go full steam ahead, like this."

Russell remains silent for what feels like an eternity, eyes downcast. Why would this question make him so uncomfortable? Usually, folks just answer, 'I want to help people.' What can of worms did I just unknowingly open?

"I'm sorry," I break the ice. "Forget I asked."

"No, its okay," he says softly. "I guess... I guess I can tell *you*." He takes a deep breath. "My mom passed away when I was little, from Crohn's Disease."

"I'm so sorry," I breathe.

"She was diagnosed at autopsy, after years of believing she just had Irritable Bowel Syndrome."

My lips part.

"After she died, my dad knew he could sue her doctors," he goes on, "since they never put her through the appropriate series of tests before settling for a diagnosis of exclusion like IBS. But, he didn't have the heart to go through with it. If I were in his shoes, I don't think I would either. It'd just be too… I dunno…" He closes his lids, temples pulsing. "So, instead," he suddenly spurts, amber eyes moist, "I decided to commit my life to preventing others from reaching the same ends. I thought about all the negligence she faced and decided I'd become the kind of doctor who'd never brush off his patients' complaints or take the easy way out when presented with a challenging case. That's what drew me to *you* in the first place; your situation reminded me so much of hers. But, at least she lived long enough to get married and have children and see those children grow a little. But, *you?* You're *so young…*"

I don't know what to say. I just sit there, holding his hand, watching his face, amazed. From the start, Russell has made our friendship all about me. He always acted like he doesn't have a single care of his own. I had no clue he's been carrying so much painful baggage, all along.

Finally, I think of something to tell him: "That's a good answer." I swallow. "You're going to be an amazing doctor."

He smiles the first real smile I've seen on his face in maybe 2 months.

"Thanks, Blanca."

BLANCA ROKITANSKY

January 4, 2010.

What a winter break this has been. I don't know if I'd really use the word 'break' to describe it.

A week before Christmas, my doctors discovered a bacterial overgrowth in my esophagus—a complication faced by most NG patients, sooner or later. As a result, I had to have my feeding tube removed. Accordingly, the weight loss resumed with a vengeance.

By now, every minute of every day, not only does my stomach feel as though stabbed with a white-hot knife, my whole body just… *aches* from head to toe. Every motion—even simple things like picking up a paperback, brushing my hair or turning on a faucet—are downright exhausting. I've resigned myself to spending my days in bed, holding my pee as long as possible so I wouldn't have to get up and walk all the way down the hall—all 10 feet of it—from my bedroom to the bathroom.

When not in bed, I practically live at Nation's Capital Hospital. I saw an orthopedic doctor who told me I have the bones of a 90-year-old. I saw a hematologist who told me I have the blood-cell-count of a cancer patient. I saw a cardiologist who told me that I'm only a couple pounds away from heart failure. And, yesterday, I saw a rheumatologist who estimated I've got 6 weeks left to live.

The moment I made it out of the hospital and into the parking lot last night, I called Russell in tears.

"Stay right where you are," he said. "I'm coming to pick you up."

"There's no need," I choked, "the metro-bus will be here in a couple minutes."

"You aren't riding back alone on my *dead body*."

I winced at his word-choice. "O-okay." I slid to my knees, right there on the slushy concrete, too tired to walk to the bench just a couple feet away. "Russell, what are we going to do? My GI still hasn't given me a diagnosis."

"Forget the GI; you need to go straight to a surgeon, like, yesterday."

"How?" I shivered violently, pants soaked with snow. "A GI has to *refer* me to a surgeon."

"There's no time for that. But, don't worry; I have a plan."

Uh oh. Not again!

RUSSELL BROWN

January 5, 2010.

Breathing shallowly, I glance left, then right. The coast is clear. No loitering nurses, orderlies, patients, nor doctors. Nervously, I begin to complete the Appointment Request Form. Patient name? *Blanca Rokitansky.* Birthdate? *06/21/89.* Immediately, her file pops up. Requested consult? *Dr. Jack Patrick.* Immediately, a window appears: 'SURGICAL CONSULT REQUIRES REFERRAL.' Twisting a curl around my index finger, I open the internet browser. I search-engine a random hospital in a random state (South Carolina) and pick a random name from their list of GIs. Then, in the 'special notes' box, I add a blurb about how the patient was tested at that facility while on winter vacation. Diagnosis? I inhale, fingers hovering over the keys.

SMA Syndrome.

BLANCA ROKITANSKY

January 7, 2010.

Russell and I don't speak much on the way to the hospital. We're both way too nervous.

"I wish you could come into the appointment with me," I murmur. "You're always so cool and calm… maybe, some of that confidence would rub off on me."

He doesn't answer.

"Your demeanor will serve you well as a doctor," I add, pensively. "It'll help prevent your patients from freaking out when you have to give them bad news."

As he rubs his lids, I notice for the first time just how very *tired* he looks. There are dark bags around his eyes that I don't remember seeing before.

"Yeah, well, something tells me they'll freak out anyway, no matter how calmly I say, 'I'm sorry, sir, ma'am, but you have a horrific, terminal illness and will spend your last months embittered and bedridden within these 4 white walls as you die a slow and painful death.'" He sighed. "I've always wanted to be a diagnostic radiologist, but now I'm not so sure. Diagnosticians tell people what's wrong with them. They drop the bomb then walk away, leaving everyone else to clean up the mess. Maybe, I should be a surgeon. At least, then, I'd actually get to *fix* the problems, not just name them."

I watch Russell cautiously from the corner of my sight. I don't like what I'm hearing. I don't like hearing my best friend say that he no longer considers his original dream to be worthwhile.

"I wish I could come with you to your appointment, too," he adds. "But, it would raise suspicions…"

"I know, I know. I'm not actually asking you to."

We enter the hospital. Cheeks burning, I study my shoes, ignoring the open guffaws from the people around me. You'd think I'd be used to all the gawking by now, since I was born albino. But, the looks I get these days are different. I used to just be an object of casual curiosity: white hair and pink eyes are not something you stumble upon everyday. Now, however, the stares were that of shock. Horror. Because, now, I'm not *just* albino. I'm a 5'5", 60-pound albino. A living ghost.

Russell heads off to his shift in Radiology as I head for the Surgical Ward. After check-in and triage, a nurse leads me to the scarlet-tinted wooden door of Dr. Jack Patrick's office.

"I'm not being seen in an examining room?" I ask the nurse. She shakes her head, eyes probing my featherlike body with barely-suppressed disgust. She knocks, pulls open the heavy door and steps aside.

To my surprise, Dr. Patrick isn't sitting at his desk in that lordly-Dr. Stuart-like-manner that I imagined he'd be— fingers folded behind a shiny gold plaque emblazoned with his name, peering at me lazily through narrow, dark-rimmed specs— but, standing only a couple paces from the entrance, smiling broadly, arm outstretched for a handshake.

"Hi there, Blanca," he says, looking at me as unflinchingly as Russell. I'm wearing my reflective shades, but he somehow still manages to meet my gaze with intensity. His eyes are bluish-grey behind frameless glasses, peering from a clean-shaven baby-face. "It's such an *honor* to meet you. Come in, let's talk about that belly of yours."

An *honor?* What peculiar word choice, considering *he's* the one with the fancy medical degree from a prestigious university, triple fellowships and a decade of experience saving lives with a scalpel. As his smile widens into a grin, I immediately feel my gut loosen and my spirits lift. I put my small, cold hand into his large, warm one—the hand that's cut into a thousand abdomens. Already, I feel safe and protected. He's nothing like Dr. Stuart.

We sit. The shelves behind him are packed with rows of thick books with impressive titles like *Pancreatic Transplantation* and *Surgical Pathology of the GI Tract*. Interspersed between the books are various framed photos of who I guess are his wife and children.

My record is already displayed on Dr. Patrick's computer, my paperwork spread across his desk.

"So, you're a freshman here at Nation's Capital," he says, pleasantly. "How are you liking college, so far? Have any idea what you want to major in, yet?"

How strange. Usually, doctors seem very rushed when they meet with me—anxious to stay on schedule, to get to their next patient, to write up a prescription for painkillers and slap a pointless follow-up appointment on their calendar. Usually, I'm out the door in under 10 minutes—before the next step of my treatment is even remotely clarified.

"I'm still deciding," I answer. "Stuck between English, Anthropology and Government. It's not possible to declare a triple, but I don't know if I can stand to pick just one when I love them all so much."

He whistles. "How about a double major and a minor?"

"Well, I'm thinking of asking the school to let me write up my own interdisciplinary curriculum."

He chuckles rhythmically, as though I just conjured the most interesting and amazing solution in the world. "What motivation you have! Most people in your health would have flunked out by now, not pursue such an intense program of study. You must be an incredible student and a brilliant young lady."

"Thank you," I breathe, face burning.

"So, your doctors in South Carolina think you have something called Superior Mesenteric Artery Syndrome," he got down to business, speaking slowly and carefully, probably assuming that I wasn't already familiar with those 4 deadly words. He raises a neat, brown brow. "They forwarded your CT images to us," he says, scrolling, "but, not the diagnostic report that normally goes with it."

Instantly, my chest flutters. I try to look surprised. "Oh?"

To my astonished relief, he just shrugs. "We get incomplete files from other facilities, all the time. Not all hospitals have a fully-digitized system like ours, and things tend to get lost in the shuffle when sent by mail or fax. So, yesterday, I just had one of our radiologists look at the scans himself." Dr. Patrick's inkjet printer hums to life. Moments later, he hands me the pages, still warm. "Dr. Michael Rethy and I agree that SMA Syndrome is indeed what you have." His blue-grey eyes are unblinking. "Your test results are undeniable. I've never seen a mesenteric angle so narrow in my decade of practice. Neither has Dr. Rethy, and he's been here for 30 years. You're only a few degrees away from complete bowel obstruction."

I feel as though I just swallowed a fistful of needles. How exactly did Dr. Patrick bring this discussion from college majors to deathly diagnoses in about 20 seconds?

"I-I really d-do have SMA S-syndrome...?" Suddenly, the room feels sweltering. Blood churns in my ears.

"Yes, Blanca," Dr. Patrick says solemnly. "I'm so sorry."

All at once, I'm stunned, relieved and horrified that Russell and I are actually right. Stunned, relieved and horrified that I am really sitting here with the Chief of Surgery, confirming a life-threatening diagnosis instead of laughing at the highly-unlikely thought. Stuff like this only happens in movies and novels. Not to real people in real hospitals. At least, not 18-year-old people.

"So, y-you do believe in it," I choke. "In the condition's existence, I mean."

It was Dr. Patrick's turn to look surprised. "You're aware of the skepticism?"

I nod, dizzy as a drunk.

"The evidence behind the validity of SMA Syndrome as a clinical entity is currently debatable, but that may change once your case gets out." His voice was incredulous. "Your scans alone could probably change the minds of the worst skeptics. If *you* don't have SMA syndrome, *no one* does."

Maybe, I'm imagining things, but now he seems almost... *happy*. Happy that I'm in this mess. Well, if what he's saying is true, he could very well get rich and famous by publishing a paper about me...

"Your case could convince the worst skeptics," he repeats, "but, it didn't *need* to convince me."

"R-really?" I spurt.

"In my opinion, there shouldn't even be a debate. SMA Syndrome is undeniable."

Those words prompt a powerful rush of gratitude toward Dr. Patrick. He's a godsend. Of all the doctors in the world, Russell managed to find me one, right here in DC, who's actually familiar with SMA Syndrome. Who's a believer.

"Your test results make it clear that, if I were to cut you open right now," he gestures sharply with his right hand, "I'd see a prominent dilation of the fist and second portions of your duodenum," he points to a barium-filled white balloon on the screen, "and a constriction of the third portion where the superior mesenteric artery lies, like a brick to a balloon." His finger shifts to the stark black spot by the white blob.

I swallow, trying not to fixate on the way he callously threw out the phrase, '*if I were to cut you open right now.*' It clashed starkly with the professional eloquence of the rest of his sentence, causing my gut to spontaneously knot up. Or, maybe, it's knotting because now I'm imagining my superior mesenteric artery as giant block of cement, flattening the circus-balloon of my intestines, threatening to tear it right open—

As if on cue, the all-too-familiar stabbing sensation returns to my upper-left belly with a vengeance; I shrink in my seat, leaning forward, feeling the golf ball bubble beneath my blouse. Dr. Patrick watches with an expression of analytical sympathy on his face.

I slide from my seat and onto the cold tile, crying open-mouthed. Moments later, my cries turn to screams.

I hear the click of phone buttons, followed by Dr. Patrick's commanding voice: "5 milligrams of IV fentanyl, stat."

In seconds, the door bangs open and a black-haired nurse in pink scrubs runs in with a syringe, roll of tape, cotton ball and alcohol wipe. While she preps a vein on my right arm, Dr. Patrick pulls on a pair of rubber gloves and takes the syringe in his hands. By this point, the pain in my belly is so consuming, I barely notice as the needle enters my skin. It's no more than a single drumbeat in my blaring symphony of agony.

Fentanyl. "A narcotic?" I whimper, once able to speak coherently. "Is that all you can do? Isn't there a medicine I could take that would actually… fix things?"

The white window-light illuminates the surgeon's crystalline eyes. "No, there is no medicine that could 'fix' you. Chronic SMA Syndrome is a mechanical obstruction. It may not be very *medically* manageable," he says, tone low and intense, "but, it is… surgically."

His chilling words seem to reverberate off the polished floor.

* * *

A quarter-hour later, I'm back in my chair, albeit in somewhat of a painkiller-induced haze.

"SMA Syndrome can present in a couple different forms," Dr. Patrick explains, "acute—as in, abruptly emerging within an inpatient stay following scoliosis surgery—and chronic—or, developing throughout the course of a lifetime and advancing due to environmental triggers, life changes, or other illnesses. Acute cases are acquired. They develop accidentally to those who would not otherwise naturally get SMA syndrome. For example, Christopher Reeve's spinal-cord injury caused the artery to tug his duodenum."

At this, my brows lift. Christopher Reeve? You'd think more people would be aware of SMA Syndrome by now if a famous person had it…!

"If Christopher Reeve never had that accident," the surgeon goes on, "he would've probably lived his entire life without ever experiencing a single SMAS symptom. Acute cases are easily treatable with medical management as opposed to surgical intervention: a feeding-tube leads to weight gain, which leads to the growth of the mesenteric fat pad, which relieves symptoms, probably forever." He leans forward. "Chronic cases, however, are genetic in origin. A person is born with certain risk factors—like a lithe frame or an unusually-short distance between the artery and the duodenum to begin with—and intermittent onsets of symptoms occur due to environmental triggers or other illnesses that cause even the slightest weight loss. Once the weight loss starts, a vicious downward spiral can ensue." He exhales, heavily. "Blanca, I believe your case is chronic, not acute. Your medical record reveals a lifelong history of abdominal complaints. When you were 8, you had a mysterious, undiagnosed 6-month episode of identical symptoms." I blink, startled to hear him spurt my history so fluently, without so much as a glance at my file. He certainly did his homework. "Obviously, the PICC line you were put on didn't cure you—it just off-set your symptoms for a few years. So, now you're back to square one, at 18. Your CT images reveal that your superior mesenteric artery emerges from your abdominal aorta only 5 or so millimeters from your duodenum, instead of the typical 10-20. You have a clear genetic predisposition—a perfect set-up for a simple seasonal flu to knock off a few crucial pounds from your already-thin frame and burn away the mesenteric fat pad holding the angle open, triggering the downward spiral into full-blown SMA Syndrome. All it takes to set off this disorder for someone with your genetic predisposition is to fail to eat properly for a few days."

"That's it?"

"That's it. Simple weight fluctuation triggers it."

"Wow," I breathe.

"Can you ensure that, every single day for the rest of your life, you will *always* eat enough and not lose a *single* pound, even if you catch a tummy bug?"

"N-no..."

His hands clasp. "My recommendation is a surgery called duodenojejunostomy." I blink. Duo-*what?* "It would bypass the constricted portion of your intestines by connecting the duodenum with the jejunum.

You'd have an unused 16-centimeter loop of bowel and an anastomosis allowing food to drop straight down instead of pumping through the constriction. This would require a midline incision of roughly 10-15 centimeters on your upper belly and at least 3 to 6 months allotted for recovery."

Whoa.

"T-that seems like a rather... invasive procedure," I babble.

He nods. "It would completely change the anatomy of your upper digestive tract. But, SMA Syndrome has already changed that anatomy. We need to work around it."

"Could we just... I don't know... wedge a synthetic fat-pad between the abdominal aorta and the SMA to keep the angle open?"

"Those are major arteries protruding from the heart. You don't operate on or around those arteries unless you have *no* other choice. It's far safer to reroute your gut. Because, if either of those arties gets *nicked,* you will instantly bleed to death on the operating table."

Holy crap. I rub my temples. "I-I need time to think."

"You don't *have* time," he presses. "Bowel obstruction is a medical emergency, Blanca. And, you don't just have *any* bowel obstruction, you have one with an extremely complex physiology. SMA Syndrome is one of the rarest gastrointestinal disorders known to medical science—the demographic is estimated at 0.013%. It isn't terminal anymore, but it still has a mortality rate of 1:3 because diagnosis is often either missed entirely, or reached after the patient has already passed the point of no return."

Silence.

"And, you think I'm close to that point." My voice quivers.

His icy blue eyes stab mine. "You're towing the line. There's a term for the kind of starvation your body is enduring—catabolysis. It's when the body begins to digest organs out of desperation for energy."

Wind leaks from my lungs.

"Not to mention," he presses on mercilessly, "every time food squeezes through your narrow mesenteric angle, you run the risk of acute gastric rupture."

"W-what's that?"

"It's when the superior mesenteric artery perforates the intestines, releasing deadly toxins into your bloodstream." He folds his arms. "You're also susceptible to developing aspiration pneumonia."

"Pneumonia?" How could a gastro-vascular disorder impact the respiratory system?

"Not pneumonia. Pneumonia is when water enters the lungs. *Aspiration* pneumonia is when *food* spasms up from the stomach and into the lungs. The first can be resolved with antibiotics. But, the latter…" He doesn't need to finish his sentence. "There's also the possibility of spontaneous upper-gastrointestinal bleeding, hypovolemic shock," he swallows, "and complete circulatory collapse. You see, the reduced mesenteric angle alters the velocity of the blood-flow in the superior mesenteric artery. The narrower the angle gets, the faster the flow. If it exceeds a certain speed, it can overtax the circulatory system, leading to its total shutdown."

I stay silent. There's no way this is real. Things like this just *don't happen* in real life. I must be watching a horror movie or reading one of those medical-thriller novels or something. Because *no one* actually stares death in the face at 18. That would go against the laws of the universe. That's not how things are supposed to *be*. Only old people—people who've had more than a couple decades of life, at the very least—can get a diagnosis like this.

"Blanca," Dr. Patrick's soft voice jolts me from my stupor, "none of this has to happen to you. I can help you before it's too late."

Surgery. Open surgery. A major bypass. Long incisions and sliced muscles and internal staples and volumes of blood loss. Oh, my goodness. Am I healthy enough to survive all that?

My head pounds. I touch my face and realize I'm crying—tears are smattering my shades.

"Is there a-any other way to treat me besides open surgery?" I choke between sobs. "Anything at all?"

"No," he answers simply, blue-grey eyes almost silver in the sterile January light filtering through the blinds.

I remove my sunglasses and put my face in my hands. "What are my chances?"

"There's no way to know for certain," his reply comes slowly, "but, considering your current state, I'd say you have… a greater than average chance of not surviving the procedure." He pulls my tear-and-mucus-smattered hand from my face, holding it gently. "But, it's the only option we have to save your life. Please, Blanca. Just give me the *honor* of trying."

RUSSELL BROWN

January 7, 2010, noon.

Just moments ago, Blanca called me on my cell to give the news.

She was formally diagnosed. Superior Mesenteric Artery Syndrome. We were right, all along.

In all my dreams to become a radiologist, I always pictured the day of diagnosis as one of victory. A day that brings newfound hope to the patient, and honor to me for solving the puzzle. But, now that this day has come for Blanca, I realize that diagnosis is not the glorious end-all-be-all that medical TV shows make it out to be. The goal isn't actually reached; the riddle is named but still unsolved. In truth, this was just the beginning of it all—the rigmarole of treatment, the fight for Blanca's life. Procedures and medications and complications. Not to mention the politics of it all—the controversy bubbling under the surface over the validity of SMA Syndrome as a real clinical entity...

I rub my temples. So, now we bought the puzzle from the game store. But, we're yet to open the box.

BLANCA ROKITANSKY

January 8, 2010, 6PM.

I collapse into bed, glad to finally be home. What a long day.

From 10AM to 5PM, I was at the hospital doing a single exam: an Upper Gastrointestinal (UGI) x-ray series, to confirm the diagnosis proposed by the CT scan.

The test began with swallowing a handful of dry carbonation crystals (ouch) to create a pocket of air in my stomach (ouch), then downing a pair of 16-ounce bottles of barium sulfate (gag) so my GI tract would show up on the x-ray. The technician, Mark, was instructed to take photos every half hour until the barium hit my colon. Right from the start, he had no reservations against expressing his displeasure with the assignment.

"Sheesh," he bellowed as he adjusted the fluoroscope, "you're tiny as they come, lady. If I'm off by a centimeter or so on a *normal* person, it would barely make a difference in the pictures. But, if I'm a centimeter off on *you,* I'll miss your whole body and wind up scanning the table."

I thought that was a rather unprofessional thing for a medical professional to say to a patient's face, but I stayed silent.

A few hours later, his tongue slipped again: "For a young, healthy individual, this test should only take a couple hours, not *all day!*"

My eyes roll. Well, if my digestive system was 'healthy,' I wouldn't have been doing the exam in the first place, now would I?

"Holy mother of Mary, what's *that?*" he suddenly spurted. I looked up at the screen and saw an enormous white cloud filling the entire field. The ballooning of my duodenum. "I'm getting backup, now."

A few minutes later, Mark returned with a couple doctors. One was a radiologist—tall, lanky and with a dark goatee. The other was a gastroenterologist—bald, round and with an expression of perpetual scorn carved into his wrinkled face. None other than Dr. Benjamin Stuart.

"You pulled me out of a departmental meeting," Dr. Stuart hissed angrily at Mark, "so, this better not be a false alarm." At that moment, his eyes landed on the screen. "What's *that?*"

"I was hoping *you'd* be able to tell *me,*" Mark said.

"It's her duodenum," the young radiologist breathed, "dilated."

Dr. Stuart's white brows lowered. "What does her chart say?"

"Superior Mesenteric Artery Syndrome," Mark answered, nervously.

The doctors exchanged a stunned glance.

"That would be consistent with the patient's lithe habitus," the radiologist spouted.

"I haven't seen a single case in my 40 years here," Dr. Stuart insisted. "Who diagnosed her?"

Mark flipped a page. "Dr. Michael Rethy."

His arms folded around his copious belly. "Should've known. Rethy's always been a nut."

"Sir," the radiologist objected.

"Dr. Haddad, there have been less than 500 recorded cases of this so-called SMA Syndrome in all of history."

There was a tense pause, followed by: "So what? Why can't she be one of them?"

I smiled.

BLANCA ROKITANSKY

January 30, 2010.

I was supposed to return to class about a fortnight ago—winter break was over. Instead, on January 13th, Russell took me to campus to empty out my dorm room. I cried the whole time we packed. It just made everything so *official,* to put my school things into boxes and give my keys to my RA and submit 'Leave of Absence Request' forms to the Dean. Official that I was too sick to be a student any longer. Official that I was dying. Official that I had a 'greater than average chance' of never coming back.

Despite the life-expectancy estimate I'd been given, my insurance company didn't allow me to have the surgery right away. I wound up having to wait 3 whole weeks; I'm going in tomorrow. The insurance company wanted to kick me off my father's plan because, as they claimed, I'm 'no longer a full-time student' now that I've declared temporary medical leave from college. Seriously.

My dad was still somewhere in Asia, but he made a few secure calls to hire a lawyer to handle the case. The health insurance company agreed to settle yesterday, allowing me to finally schedule my operation, but only after wasting 3 precious weeks—half my life expectancy.

All month, I've been in a strange fog. I'm glad for the numbness because it's certainly better than the anxiety and terror I always believed I would feel upon facing death. I realized that I'm just afraid of pain, not death itself. I interpret the peace as a gift from God. There's no other possible explanation than a supernatural one, because the Blanca I know would normally go crazy at a time like this. But, instead, I feel… almost nothing. I thought a lot about heaven and eternity since my diagnosis and was surprised to discover that I actually don't mind dying, all that much. Dying would end the continual pain, after all. Heaven will be so much better than this. A few Sundays ago, my pastor talked about the 'glorified bodies' we'll have in New Jerusalem. My glorified body surely won't have a narrow mesenteric angle, a demolished immune system, hollowed bones or an atrophied heart. My glorified body won't feel the need to vomit every bite, or cry when my blouse brushes my tummy the wrong way. My glorified body will have enough muscle mass to walk—no, to *run,* and to leap.

Of course, there's still a large part of me that isn't ready to give up this waking nightmare. A large part of me that wants to live. I'm my mom's whole family, after all. Without me, she'll be totally alone. And, then, there's Russell. Our friendship isn't even a year old—I'm not ready to give it up, quite yet.

Russell is back in school, but he visits most nights to keep me company while doing his homework. As if on cue, the doorbell rings now.

"How did your bio lab go?" I ask the moment I yank open the door, panting a little from the exertion.

He shrugs. "Eh, not too well." Unwinding his scarf, he shakes the snow from his curly hair. "I swear, the professor always gives me *the* fattest cadavers to autopsy. Everyone else had clean cuts and easy organ-access, while I was stuck wasting half the class-period pushing aside handfuls of blubber. Thin people are *so* much easier to operate on!"

"I guess my surgeon is going to love me, then," I laugh.

"I-I'm sorry," he sputtered. "I didn't mean to bring up—"

"That's okay; don't worry about it." We scuttle to the living-room.

"How was your pre-op?"

"My freak-show exhibit, you mean?" My eyes roll. "Basically, I was ogled by throngs of Dr. Patrick's students, interns and colleagues, and asked the same questions over and over: 'What positions help relieve the pain?' 'Leaning forward.' 'Ahh, yes, that's consistent with SMA Syndrome. That opens the mesenteric angle, you know.' 'Yes, I know.' 'Where does it hurt?' 'Right here, my upper-left belly.' 'Yes, yes, there's where the dilation and constriction are.' 'When did your symptoms begin?' 'How much did you weigh before symptoms?' 'How much do you weigh, now?' 'What are you able to eat?' And, on and on and on. I feel like a museum artifact, or a zoo animal."

Russell shrugs again. "Hey, if it helps spread awareness of your rare condition. After your case, skeptics will have a harder time denying SMA Syndrome's validity as a clinical entity."

One could only hope.

BLANCA ROKITANSKY

January 31st, 3:30PM.

I feel surreally calm as I'm wheeled into the cold operating room, numerous pairs of eyes following me. I don't know when it happened, but at some point, I must have signed a consent form permitting Dr. Patrick's massive posse to watch, and for the entire procedure to be videotaped for 'instructional purposes.' I'm the hospital's very first duodenojejunostomy.

I also had to sign a special form for the immunocompromised that stated, 'I understand I have a greater than average chance of not surviving through this procedure.' They waited until about 5 minutes ago—*after* bringing me into the prep area and starting the IVs—before presenting me with *that* document. Yeah.

As I'm lifted up onto the high table, my eyes scan the room, glittering with the lights of various machines. I'm completely naked under the towels, and it's very chilly. But, I'm too numb to shiver.

Powerful lights loom over my head, only inches away. I turn and behold the sea of masked faces, covered heads and green scrubs. I recognize Dr. Patrick's ice-blue eyes. Approaching slowly, he gives me a re-assuring wink before placing a plastic gas-mask over my mouth and nose.

"Blanca, could you please count backward from 10 for me?" he asks gently.

"10…" I speak aloud, into the mask.

Lord Jesus? I plead, silently.

"9…"

Even now, Lord.

"8…."

You are good to me.

"7…."

Even now—

The world is black.

PART II

*"Cutting-edge medical researchers
now believe that
life and death
begin in the digestive tract."*

—Jordan Rubin, N.M.D., Ph.D.,
in *The Maker's Diet*

BLANCA ROKITANSKY

February 1, 2010.

I awake to the worst pain of my life. It's worse than the farthest reaches of what I ever imagined pain could be. I can't believe I'm even conscious. Surely, I'd pass out from the agony? Throat is closing. Tummy is swollen. Scar is wide and maroon-colored and frightening, like something out of a Halloween horror flick. They wipe it with this strange yellow-orange goo then cover it with a bandage. There are a couple enormous tubes down my nose, each quite a bit thicker than a feeding tube. One goes into my stomach, and the other, my lungs. Sharp pains shoot up my bladder, too—I'm hooked to a catheter. A little bag of pale-yellow urine hangs by my feet. They roll me down a hall and to a private room, and now they want me to get up and switch beds. Can't. There's no way I can move. So, they lift me on the sheet. Tell me to roll over on my side. Can't bear the thought of lying on anything but my back—stomach is too sensitive. Someone sticks a huge needle in my right hand, attached to an IV. Hands me a button I can push every 8 minutes for narcotic pain relief. I press down hard and my head starts spinning.

* * *

February 2, 2010.

Awakening in a panic, I rip the tubes from my nose. Now, I'm suffocating without the respirator. Machines all around my head start beeping loudly and a bunch of nurses in patterned scrubs burst into my room with a 'crash cart.' They stuff 2 new tubes back into my face forcibly. It's so painful, I black out.

When I wake up again, I hear a voice telling me to get up and walk. Walking is supposed to help prevent blood-cots. But, I still can't get up. The tubes keep sliding from my nostrils, lubricated by a trickle of my own blood and mucus, thick like ketchup. They change the spouts, securing them with plenty of tape across my face. An hour later, the tape gives way and the pipes start sliding again, renewing the slimy nosebleed.

* * *

February 3, 2010.

I still can't stand the sensation of my own gown brushing my belly. I spent the last few days holding it up, when conscious. Legs are inside giant pumps. Sticky, sweaty, plastic-lined pumps. They are supposed to help keep my blood circulating so a clot won't form and suddenly stop my heart. Stand up, they say. Walk, they say. I shakily get to my feet, leaning against my IV pole. The pain is so bad when walking, I faint and hear the thud of my own head hitting the tile.

* * *

February 4, 2010.

Concussion.

* * *

February 5, 2010.

Nurse adds a large bag of formula to my IV pole, making it very top-heavy. She accidentally elbows the stand and it pitches over, yanking the tube right out of my nose. Blood and goo spurt onto the floor.

"We're going to need an orderly in here," she says into the intercom.

90 minutes later, Russell comes in with a mop. His eyes are moist and red as they move back and forth from the blotchy floor to my bloodstained face.

* * *

February 6, 2010.

Respirator and tummy-tube removed. Breaths are shallow. Like suffocating. Not allowed anything by mouth yet, not even water—status called 'NPO.' Nurse swabs my throat with wet sponge, but I'm not allowed to swallow. Must spit everything, even saliva. Nurse sticks what looks like a giant inhaler in my mouth, tells me to exhale as hard as I can. "Incentive spirometer," she calls it. It's a breathing exercise, so my lungs can properly function without the respirator. I'm supposed to see how far I can make the lever rise. I'm supposed to send it to the top. I blow and blow but it barely rises an inch. Lungs sear and burn, almost as bad as my belly.

* * *

February ??

I can't keep track of date or time anymore. A huge snowstorm hit the east coast. People are calling it the 'Snowpocalypse of 2010.' Over 30 inches.

* * *

February ???

I wish my surgeon a good morning; he tells me its 9PM. Wonder what he's still doing here. Probably snowed in. I saw some happy college students outside my window earlier, laughing, chatting and playing in the winter wonderland. I wonder why I have to be in here while they get to be out there.

* * *

February ????

Russell visits a lot. Not sure how often; I still can't get a handle on the whole day-and-night thing.

A few others from school come with Russell to see me today. They act super nice, the kind of nice that people act when something really screwed-up has happened and they're trying to put a happy face on some real bad stuff.

* * *

February ?????

New nurse I've never seen before 'takes care' of me today. Says she wants to give me my daily heparin shot either in my stomach or my arm. Doesn't bother to check my chart to see that my belly clearly isn't an option. I must insist. 4 times. She sticks me anyway. I scream.

* * *

February 10, 2010, 6:21PM.

Mom brought me my phone so I can finally keep track of how long I've been in this hell-hole. 10 days so far. Feels more like 10 years.

* * *

February 11, 2010, 5:02AM.

Time for a chest x-ray. Technician comes in, doesn't check my chart. Drops the lead shield right on my incision. I scream.

* * *

February 13, 2010, 9:04PM.

This morning, around 10AM, my new roommate accidentally pooped on the floor. She pushed the call button, asked for it to get cleaned up. 11 hours later, it's still here.

* * *

February 14, 2010, 7:24PM

Today isn't so bad, after all. Russell just brought me roses.

* * *

February 15, 2010, 6:07PM.

It's like my body is covered in mosquito bites. The burning itch is unbearable. I writhe in my bedsheets, panting and crying. My finger slams the call button, repeatedly.

A full hour later, a nurse hooks me to a hydroxyzine drip. Apparently, I'm allergic to the morphine Dr. Patrick recently switched me to (couldn't stay on fentanyl indefinitely, thanks to the risk of addiction). Within seconds of starting the IV, my world goes black.

I finally awaken, groggy and nauseous, to the blurry sight of the nurse bending over me.

"How much did you say you weighed, again?" she croaks.

"Around 60 pounds, I think," I murmur.

"Oh! If I'd known, I wouldn't have given you so much hydroxyzine—stuff knocked you right out!"

Um, you didn't think to check my chart before shooting me up!?

* * *

February 16, 2010, 6:06PM.

Dr. Patrick comes by my room and tells me, "I know you well, inside and out."

Creepy much?

* * *

February 17, 2010, 2:00AM.

I can't sleep. I hear voices outside my room door—a pair of interns, I think—talking about some dirty movie they saw the other night. And, they aren't holding anything back, either; I'm gleaning just about everything that the blonde chick did to the bald dude. My lids crack open as I peek at the chair by the foot of my bed, and sure enough, I see mom's silhouette against the pale moonlight filtering through the blinds. Sometimes, when she visits me after finishing up her late work-shift, she winds up falling asleep in her seat and spending half the night in my room before a nurse discovers her and kicks her out.

My whole health fiasco is really putting mom on-edge; she's far more irritable these days than normal. It doesn't take much to set her off. I see her head turn toward the door; she's awake. Uh oh. She throws the door open. I pull my blanket over my head.

"Excuse me!" she explodes in her heavy Spanish accent. "This is the surgical ward in a HOSPITAL! It's the middle of the night and the patients are trying to SLEEP! We can't have you two talking loudly about PE-NISES AND VAGINAS in the hall, right outside their doors!"

My jaw literally drops. Ohmygosh. What did she just say!?

"Well, if anyone just woke up the patients, it's you," the guy answers.

"We're sorry, ma'am," the girl laughs. "We'll keep it down. By the way, visitation hours are over—what are you still doing here?"

* * *

February 21, 2010, 7:24AM.

Discharged. Can't believe I'm making it out alive.

BLANCA ROKITANSKY

March 24, 2010.

I had a rather interesting post-op appointment, this morning. Dr. Stuart told me that my UGI and CT images were reviewed in a large hospital-wide conference, a couple days ago. The topic of discussion? The *existence* of SMA Syndrome. I mean, I know Dr. Stuart has always been a skeptic himself, but lo and behold, today he told me he's now willing to consider that SMAS 'may be real,' for my images are a 'most compelling example.'

Sheesh, 'bout time.

* * *

May 4, 2010.

The last couple months passed in a flurry of checkups and scans. I've gotten quite friendly with the x-ray machines.

"I've been injected and fed so many radioactive chemicals this year, I think I might turn into an x-woman, any day now," I tell Russell, now.

"What's your special power?" he chortles.

I chew my lip for a moment. "The ability to attract a very large number of confused doctors."

PART III

*"Doctors are men who prescribe medicine
of which they know little,
to cure diseases of which they know less,
to human beings
of whom they know nothing."*

—*Voltaire*

BLANCA ROKITANSKY

January 7, 2011.

I remember

the delivery of those four words

one year ago today

    ending in *syndrome*

the pale silver-grey

of the doctor's eyes as he spoke

monotonously

Life-threatening

the black and white stripes of my jacket

the one with the broken

zipper

Only five-hundred cases—

> *in history*

the tacky leftover Christmas

wreath on the auburn

wooden office door

> *Invasive surgery*

or six weeks left

> *to live*

the sunken

cheeks, sallow

skin and dead

eyes of a sixty-pound eighteen-year-old

staring at me from the

mirror

behind his desk

Slim chance of survival

patches of straggly

white hair framing my angular jaw

Sign here please

the ten-degree wind

whipping

my as face I left

the hospital

        floating

too numb

     for fear

BLANCA ROKITANSKY

It's been a year since my diagnosis and sadly, the terrain has grown rocky once more. After a couple months of relatively normal life—during which I excitedly prepared to return to college for the spring 2011 semester—I've begun to experience recurrent SMA Syndrome symptoms. None of my local physicians could explain why.

So, yesterday, I applied for a diagnostic session at the renowned Musta Clinic down in Jacksonville, Florida. This morning, they got back to me. I was alarmed; Musta applicants aren't accepted on a first-come-first-serve basis, but according to the team's evaluation of the severity of each patient's condition, based off the submitted medical history reports.

My session was scheduled to begin on January 28th, which is barely more than 2 weeks away. Yikes. I must be in trouble.

RUSSELL BROWN

January 28, 2010, 7AM. The shrill of the alarm clock pierces my consciousness.

This morning, Blanca is checking into the Musta Clinic. Yesterday, she and her mom road-tripped 800 miles to Jacksonville, all in one go.

Today is 'SMA Syndrome Awareness Day' at Nation's Capital University. One funny thing about college students: they're some of the most easily-excitable people on earth, ever searching for a novel cause to throw themselves behind—or, at the very least, a reason to wave signs in the quad and wear special outfits to class. Colleges are inevitably populated by rebel-wannabies with wild internal compasses, perpetually spinning in search of a new North.

It all started with my telling the Pre-Med Club that my best friend is checking into the Musta Clinic on January 28th due to a relapse of her extremely-rare disorder. I was just hoping for some words of comfort and reassurance, but upon discovering that her condition isn't even recognized by the National Organization of Rare Conditions (NORC), my peers conjured up some bigger ideas to run away with. Eager to root for the 'underdog,' these doctor-wannabies spontaneously decided to start an awareness campaign for her condition around campus, collecting signatures from students and professors so that they may eventually petition NORC to include SMA Syndrome in their database of research endeavors. Through social-networking websites, endless email-forwarding-chains, flyering and chalking, the idea for an awareness day spread across Nation's Capital University like wildfire. Today, participants are showing solidarity by wearing shirts or ribbons of the same color—purple.

* * *

It's only noon now, but the online event already has over 2,000 RSVPs and a gallery of nearly 600 photos of random students wearing purple shirts or holding signs bearing slogans like 'SMA SYNDROME: NOT

TOO RARE TO CARE!' or 'PRAYING FOR BLANCA TODAY!'

I'm sure a good number of these people never even met Blanca.

Honestly, I don't wish she were here to see all this. I just wish she never had the deadly disorder that's giving these rebels a cause in the first place.

RUSSELL BROWN

January 28, 2011, 8PM. My shift is over, thank heavens. I've been itching to call Blanca, all day. I bolt out the door.

"Hey," I blurt, the moment she picks up, "can you talk now? Where are you—still in the hospital or back at the hotel? Are you alright? Is everything okay? What tests did you have? What did the doctors say? What's the Musta Clinic like?"

"And, hello to you, too, Russell," she chortles, tiredly. "Slow down, there, buddy."

"So, did they find out what's wrong with you?" I press.

"They sure did."

"And?"

"And, I have SMA Syndrome."

Pause.

"Okay... what?"

"Uh huh, that's what they did with me today: run a series of tests to re-diagnose me with SMA Syndrome."

Snow crunches beneath my boots. "You've got to be kidding me. Are they going to re-verify your albinism, too? Do some chemical and genetic testing to make sure your hair isn't white from bleach?"

She chuckles. "Russell, SMAS may seem obvious to *us*, but we can't forget the skeptics. There's a fair share of them out here, too."

"Really?" Despite the 20° chill, I plop down under a tree in the quad. Skepticism. Of all places in the world, I wouldn't expect the top hospital in the nation to have *that* problem.

"Yes. This afternoon, one radiologist actually said, straight to my face, 'well, no one *truly* knows if SMA Syndrome is a valid clinical entity.' I fought the urge to say something along the lines of, 'Really? How about I kick you in the stomach, and then you can tell me if *that* feels legit?'"

I laugh hard, because I know that's the reaction Blanca wants, though the whole situation really isn't funny in the least.

BLANCA ROKITANSKY

January 29, 2010, 5AM. I awake in my hotel bed, screaming from outrageous (even for me) abdominal pain. Mom and I decide to head for the Musta ER.

This is only our second day in Jacksonville—we're still fairly unfamiliar with the area. And so, mom turns on her car's incredibly-chattery, glitch-ridden, clunky, screenless GPS.

"Good morning," comes a robotic female voice. "Welcome to One-Sun E-Navigation. Let me connect you. Or, say, 'No thanks.'"

A lengthy pause ensues.

"*Por cielo*, just hurry up!" mom shouts.

"I'm listening, now. Please say the name of your stored destination—"

"Musta Clinic!"

"Or, if you cannot remember the name of your stored destination, please say 'list,' and I will gladly list everything I have stored in the system."

"I said, 'Musta Clinic'!"

"Slower, please."

"*Musta Clinic!*"

"I'm sorry; I didn't get that. Could you please repeat for me the name of your stored destination? Or, if you cannot remember it, please say 'list' and I will gladly—"

"TAKE ME TO THE EL HOSPITAL, *MALDITO!*"

"Pardon? I'm listening, now. Please say the name of your stored destination. Slowly, please."

"Muuussstaaaa Cliiiinnnniiic!"

After a painfully-long pause, the GPS finally replies, "Got it. You said, 'Musta Clinic.' Is that correct? Please say, 'yes' or—"

"YES!"

"Or say, 'no.'"

"I SAID, YES!"

Yet another silence.

"*¡Adelantado!*"

"Thank you. Please wait while directions are sent to your vehicle. You may cancel your route at any time. To do so, just push the hands-free call button and say 'cancel route.' Thank you and goodbye."

"It's about time, *maldición!*" mom reels, taking the wrong way out of the parking lot.

"You have left the highlighted route," the electronic voice returns. "Would you still like directions to your destination—"

"Yes!"

"Or, should I cancel your route? I'm listening, now. Please say, 'yes' to get directions or 'no' to cancel your route."

"YES! *¡Sí!*"

* * *

Eventually, we manage to make it to the hospital where I'm given IV Vicodin. Then, a nurse comes in to shave my privates for an angiogram; yep, I'm about to have a system of wires and contrast-agent-loaded catheters threaded from my groin to my femoral artery, to image my abdominal arterial tree. The purpose? To measure the exact degree of my mesenteric angle. Then, afterward, I'm going to have a hida-scan to check my gallbladder's ejection-fraction, followed by an endoscopy to take a look at the surgical site with a tiny camera.

Nothing like an extensive internal-photo-shoot to pass the day.

* * *

A young cardiologist in an oversized white coat overtop stained blue scrubs walks into the examining room with a tragically-somber face, holding a clipboard. Uh oh. I know that look all too well, by now...

He begins by explaining that the angiogram indicates dangerously-increased blood-flow in my superior mesenteric artery due to the reduced aortal-mesenteric angle, overtaxing the heart and putting me at risk of sudden circulatory collapse.

"What can be done about it?" I ask, placidly.

"I'd like to give you an intravenous blood-thickener and take an ultrasound to see if the med brings you down to the normal range. It's an experimental idea; we haven't seen a case quite like yours, before. But, I'd like to give medical management a shot before calling for a surgical consult."

2 hours and 6 needle-pricks later, I'm in the ICU with mesenteric thrombosis. That's right—a bloodclot in my superior mesenteric artery, just inches below my heart. I swung straight from one extreme to the other. The doctors in the ICU give me IV heparin to thin my blood, then take another ultrasound to verify I'm clotless and

back to square one, dangerously-increased blood-flow-velocity perfectly restored. The cardiologist hands me a printout of the test results without a word of apology for having nearly killed me with his stupid idea.

30 minutes later, a gastroenterologist named Dr. Jose Albin strolls in.

"The hida scan shows that your gallbladder, though functioning at the lowest possible capacity, is *still functioning*, so removal is not a necessity," he says. "With attention to nutrition labels, it can be managed. Now, yesterday's gastric-emptying lab shows delayed motility, which can be treated with metoclopramide. The blood-draws show hepatic steatosis, hemocytosis, leucopenia and hypotension, your EKG shows mild chronic tachycardia, and your dexa-scan shows osteoporosis of the lumbar spine and osteopenia of the femoral hip."

I stare blankly, all the fancy medical terminology congealing in my mind. Say, what?

"All of these are the body's natural responses to severe malnutrition, set off by the SMA Syndrome. So, if we take care of the SMA Syndrome and return you to a healthy weight, all of these complications will spontaneously resolve." He took a deep breath. "Now, the reason your SMA Syndrome is returning... is due to a significant buildup of scar tissue at the surgical site."

I freeze.

"The anastomosis is clogged by a clearly visible grid of tissues," he continues. "You have external adhesions as well; your bowels are sticking to the abdominal wall, explaining your visceral hypersensitivity."

My lips part. "Scar tissue? H-how did that happen?"

Dr. Albin swallows. "Blanca, your duodenojejunostomy was performed fully open, is that correct?"

I nod.

"I must ask," his throat clears, "why did your surgeon in DC recommend that course of action, when such a procedure could've easily been performed laparoscopically?"

"Laparoscopically?" I echo the unfamiliar term.

"Most procedures that do not involve the transit of large pieces of matter—as with transplants—can be performed with a few small punctures rather than a long incision. A laparoscopic surgeon operates using tiny cameras and tools threaded through these punctures. That way, several of the complications that are endemic to open surgery are avoided, including the possibility of nerve damage, high volume of blood-loss and future adhesion development. Recovery time and narcotic use are also reduced by more than 50%. Overall, laparoscopy is far less traumatic to the body. For someone in your delicate health, it would've been a much safer and more effective option. About 4% of abdominal laparoscopic procedures result in adhesion development within a year or so after surgery. But, with open operations, that percentage jumps to 94. One significant factor that contributes to adhesion growth is exposure to the open air—organs are more likely to dry out when a large incision is made as opposed to a few tiny punctures, even if the team irrigates frequently. Also, open surgeries involve sponging, as there tends to be spillage. That kind of manipulation also greatly increases adhesion-risk." His arms fold. "I don't understand why your surgeon would put you through all that when the alternative is obvious."

My jaw is hanging openly, now. I feel as though all half-dozen hospital floors are collapsing onto my head, at this very moment.

"H-he told me I had n-no other choice," I sputter. "I asked him if there was another way, and h-he said no."

Dr. Patrick is the Chief of the Nation's Capital Department of Gastrointestinal Surgery; there's no way he couldn't have known that laparoscopy was an option for me!

Of course. Pieces fall into place, in my mind. Dr. Patrick is primarily a *transplant* surgeon. He doesn't typically perform laparoscopic procedures. He would've had to refer me to someone else, giving up the prestigious opportunity to perform an extremely-rare operation on a patient with a largely-unknown disease.

"I never thought I'd encourage a patient to do this," Dr. Albin's troubled voice interrupts my thoughts, "but, I think you have substantial matter for a lawsuit. What your surgeon did was a blatant violation of the Hippocratic Oath. He withheld crucial information, choosing not to do what is in *your* best interest as his patient, but what is in the best interest of his career."

I put my face in my hands. The care, the concern, the charm, the constant reminders of what an *honor* it was to treat me… all an act? Was Dr. Patrick's irresistible charisma just a tool to get me to consent to his next career-bolstering move?

An enormous lump rises in my throat. I'm not a *person* to Dr. Patrick, just a new line on his resume. I can't believe it. SMA Syndrome is supposed to be the only 'bad guy' here. The *disease* is the enemy, while the doctors are supposed to be the good guys. They're supposed to be on my side. But now, the world is spinning backward.

"I-I'm going to need surgery again, aren't I?" I choke, vision blurring.

"Yes," Dr. Albin answers solemnly. "Gastrointestinal surgery is the only way we can clear your abdomen of the adhesions that have been triggering your relapse—with the anastomosis choked, you have been forced to rely on the old constricted loop of bowel. If we don't operate right away, you'll deteriorate back to the state you were in this time last year, and eventually die."

BLANCA ROKITANSKY

February 3, 6:04PM. The eve of my second operation. I'm spending the day in my hotel room, prepping.

INCOMING CALL, my cell screen flashes, *RUSSELL BROWN.* For the umpteenth time today, I push 'ignore.' Then, I lift my eleventh cup of 'Go-Lightly' pre-op cleanser to my lips (no joke, that really is the name of the drink), pinch my nose and take a sip. I shudder as the sour liquid burns its way down my throat and slams into my empty belly like a block of lead. Dr. Albin instructed me not to consume anything but 6 liters of this gag-inducing chemical starting from 12:00AM today until the surgery at 3:30PM tomorrow.

The best way to describe 'Go-Lightly' is: laxatives on steroids. Designed to sweep your bowels clean from tummy to colon in a mere handful of hours, the stuff has me literally pooping clear water, all day long.

Russell and I have talked every evening since I arrived in Jacksonville. I usually contact him the second I'm through with the day's consultations, as I'm leaving the hospital for the hotel. But, since last night, I've refused to answer any of his calls.

I halt in mid-gulp and make a break for the bathroom, once again. Sitting on the cold toilet seat, my chest constricts like the winter I weathered pneumonia, acid smolders in my abdomen and goosebumps grip my arms—like someone is pulling my body's fire alarm. I run my fingers through my tangled hair and find my forehead a stovetop. Shivers zip from my pelvic bone to my neck. I lean forward and put my cheeks in my palms, examining the bits of hair and dust in the grey grout of the tiles. Then, I feel a mighty rush exit my body, freakishly odorless and transparent.

20 minutes later, I'm curled up in a fetal position, in bed. Mom is out grabbing a fast-food dinner. I check my phone and determine that it's time for yet another draught of cleanser. The very thought makes me want to cry. But, I don't have the energy for tears.

As I'm pouring myself another malodorous cup, I hear my cell blare again. When I'm back in bed, full glass in hand, I glance at the screen and see that, this time, I missed a call from mom. Great. Now, she's going to think I've passed out in the bathroom or something, and she'll come rushing back in a panic. Better return her call ASAP.

I put the cup down and flip open the phone—but, a split second prior, another call came in. Russell.

I accidentally answered him.

"Blanca?" his frazzled voice emits from the receiver. "Blanca, are you there?"

In spite of myself, I sigh and put the cell to my cheek. "Hey," I say, coldly.

"Blanca," he breathes, "is everything okay? What happened? Why haven't you been answering your phone? You have me worried *sick,* over here!"

"Sorry," I retort, voice low.

"What's going on? Is everything okay?" he repeats.

"Well, actually, no, Russell," I growl, "everything's *not* okay. You see, I'm having surgery tomorrow," I drop the bomb.

There's a stunned pause, followed by—
"What? You mean, like a PICC-line place-
ment or something?"

"No, it's not an outpatient procedure like
that. My belly's going to get sliced open, all
over again."

"*What?* Why?"

I abruptly launch into Dr. Albin's explanation, and when I finish, the world's loud-
est silence ensues.

"I-I can't believe it," Russell finally sputters. "I'm *so* sorry, I didn—"

"Yeah, well, you should be sorry," my voice
cracks, "because you're the one who set me
up with Dr. Patrick, in the first place."

"Well, Blanca," he says, "Dr. Patrick is the
Chief of the Department; I *thought* I was
giving you the best of the best. I didn't want
to settle for anything less—"

"You never had the right to give me a referral in the first place, Russell!" I explode.
"You're not my doctor. You're not *a* doctor!"

"Blanca, please—"

I snap the cell shut.

BLANCA ROKITANSKY

Déjà-vu overwhelms me as I lay upon the icy operating table, paying no mind to the nurse repeatedly mis-sticking my veins, her attempts marked by black blotches pooling just below my translucent skin.

"I'm willing to try again if you are," she says sheepishly after her fourth failed attempt.

"Go right ahead," I say unflinchingly. "I'm desensitized to needles."

"I've noticed!" she breathes, laughingly.

Dr. Albin marches in, followed by a pack of assistants all dressed in green scrubs, white hair-coverings, yellow facemasks and purple gloves. I scrunch my lids shut.

Moments later, I feel the touch of a gas-mask against my face. I take a long draught and begin counting backward from 10 before Dr. Albin could ask.

I know the drill.

BLANCA ROKITANSKY

"Hey, I think she's coming around!"

"Blanca? *Blanca?*"

"Shhh!"

"Blanca?"

Slowly, my 2-ton lids lift. A russet-and-purple-colored blur hovers over me.

"Hmm?" I breathe, headache pounding. Someone chuckles and slides my glasses up my nose.

I watch as Russell's sweat-sprinkled face breaks into a dimpled grin. He's wearing a dark-purple shirt, flanked by maybe 2-dozen other purple shirts. I turn my stiff neck, hair falling onto my pillow. I'm in my bed, in my room… at home. Surrounded by throngs of students from school. Students holding flowers and balloons.

What?

"Welcome home," Russell breathes. "Boy, am I glad to see you! Though I doubt the feeling's mutual…" his voice trails.

Huh? Why wouldn't I be glad to see my best friend? My best friend who saved my life. I wouldn't be here today if he didn't forcibly interject in my case, back in high school. Why did I ever get angry at him? I mean, there's no way he could've known who or *what* Dr. Patrick really is. Plus, deception and complications aside, Dr. Patrick's work still saved my life, in the long run. In January of 2009, I was told I had 6 weeks to live. And, yet, here I still am, over a year later.

"I'm sorry for yelling," I murmur to Russell.

He shrugs, smile widening. "It's okay. You were under a lot of stress; I understand."

"I think I finally understand, too," I whisper, "why your family never sued your mom's doctors. I don't want to sue *him* either. There's a better way to go about making up for… everything."

He chuckles. "You want to become a doctor?"

What? "No way." I give him a mischievous grin. "I have a totally different idea."

BLANCA ROKITANSKY

March 3, 2011.

Since Musta is 800 miles away, I obviously can't see Dr. Albin for my post-ops. So, today, I'm returning to Nation's Capital… to a surgeon who *isn't* Dr. Patrick.

I walk into Dr. Green's office now, shake his hand and sit down, guard automatically up. I don't know if I'll ever feel comfortable around surgeons again.

"Judging from this operative report," Dr. Green begins, "I'd say the team down at the Musta Clinic did everything in their power to reduce the risk of future adhesion redevelopment—"

The office door suddenly bursts open with a spectacular creak. Framed in the doorway is none other than Dr. Jack Patrick, pale face void of his signature charismatic glow. Immediately, my chest constricts as cold sweat issues from every pore in my body. I can practically feel his icy aura lift the hairs on my arms with a prickle.

"Hi there," he says, voice hard.

"Good afternoon, Chief," Dr. Green replies with a plastered grin.

I bite down on my lip so hard, it bleeds.

"I see you have *my* patient, here," Dr. Patrick continues. "As you may be aware, Dr. Green, it is the policy at Nation's Capital for patients to remain under the care of the same physician. I operated on Blanca, last year—a duodenojejunostomy for Superior Mesenteric Artery Syndrome."

"My apologies, Chief," Dr. Green stands and hands Dr. Patrick my chart, "I'll just leave you at it, then." He scuttles out, closing the door behind him.

I can't breathe. Hell no. This isn't happening.

"Abdominal adhesions, huh?" Dr. Patrick murmurs, blue-grey eyes sweeping the clipboard. "I'm sorry, but that isn't possible for the type of procedure I performed."

Not possible? Then what exactly did the Musta Clinic operate on? Heat rushes to my cheeks.

"Sir," I breathe quietly, "I respect the hospital's policies, but if being a patient at

Nation's Capital means entrusting my case to you alone," I swallow, "then I'm through with Nation's Capital, as a whole."

And, with that, I rise to my feet and float out into the hall.

RUSSELL BROWN

April 7, 2011, 5PM.

There comes a knock on my dorm window. Blanca is back from her appointment at Farris Hospital in Northern Virginia.

I yank open the door. "Hey! How did everything go, today?"

"You won't believe this," she says dryly, coming in. "Dr. Yinrale wants to take out my gallbladder." She kicks off her tiny shoes. "Surprise, surprise. A surgeon wants me to have surgery."

"Your gallbladder? Why?"

"In his words, 'because it tends to cause people problems.'" Exhaling heavily, she plops down on my bed. "I told him that my doctors at Musta specifically advised against it. My ejection fraction is *fine* and the last thing I need now is more surgery when everything is still so *raw,* down there."

"What did Dr. Yinrale say to that?"

"He made a joke: 'The appendix was created so surgeons can send their first child to college. The gallbladder was created so surgeons can send their second child to college.'"

"No way," I gape. "You've got to be kidding me." Bedside manner at its finest.

"Nope." She chuckles. "But, at least quotes like Dr. Yinrale's are literary gold."

I blink. "What?"

She only smiles.

BLANCA ROKITANSKY

June 21, 2012. The summer solstice. The longest day of the year. My twentieth birthday. About a year and a half since my corrective operation.

I turn on the bathroom faucet, duck my head in the sink and toss a handful of cool water in my eyes. Then, I look up at my reflection in the mirror and smile at the face that's becoming rosier and rounder, every day.

Russell has his medical career cut out for him. As my story got discovered by television shows and magazines, he became famous for suggesting my initial diagnosis and risking everything to run the scan (now published in the *World Journal of Gastroenterology*) that wound up saving my life. Already, med schools were throwing themselves at him.

As for me, I wrote a novel about a fictional college girl named Samantha who battled SMA Syndrome. Within a single week of publication, my so-called 'medical thriller' hit the local bestseller list. To be perfectly honest, the book's plot is a little toned down from what actually happened to me; I figured there was no way the average reader would accept the whole truth.

Reality is stranger than fiction, that's for sure.

EPILOGUE

Dear Blanca,

I am a 58-year-old women living in Salt Lake City, Utah. I have suffered more mis-diagnoses regarding my illness than I can remember. Recently, multiple tests confirm I have SMA Syndrome, Nutcracker Syndrome and Pelvic Congestion. I'm relieved to finally have a diagnosis that makes sense; but frightened about where I go from here.

I am so grateful for your research and dedication to spreading the word. I actually took a printout of your research on the online encyclopedia to my last emergency visit to help them understand how to help me. Finding your online support group was an answer to my prayers. I was hoping to find someone else with this illness and was very surprised to find an actual support group with so many members.

Thank you for sharing your story with me and others so we might be spared the horrific traumas you have suffered. It deeply saddens me that you have gone through so much to bring this knowledge to light. I am very grateful for your bravery, intelligence, and endurance. I felt so alone until I met you. Now, because of your good works and experience, I am comforted. You are an inspiration to us all. I intend to make an appointment with my vascular specialist and discuss my options. The older I get the worse the flare-ups. I feel it's time to finally take a different approach. You've given me the information to begin talks with the surgeon.

Thank you so much.

S. C.

* * *

Dear Blanca,

You are an inspiration to us all! Your courage and gracious acceptance of the ebb and flow of this menacing disease inspires those of us going through similar experiences. Bless you for sharing your experiences. The world needs to know this is a complicated, challenging and complex disease. As you know by sharing your experience the word is spreading. You give us all hope. May you find peace in knowing you have helped so many others though sharing your experiences.

I'm grateful for all the information you've given me, like about the antispastic meds. I intend to discuss that idea with my pain management team when I see them. I hadn't given it much thought until you mentioned it.

Thanks!

M. C.

* * *

Dear Blanca,

Have I told you lately how much I appreciate you? I feel so blessed to have someone who understands this "syndrome" and helps me keep it in perspective. I pray for your continued recovery. We all bless you for the work you have done and continue to do. You are blazing the trail for the future of SMA syndrome survivors, whether you know it or not. Thank God for your courage and abilities to express yourself. Knowing you has lightened my load considerably. Thank you from the depths of my heart.

Because of you, I'm not afraid of this syndrome anymore. Thank you so much for all you've done and do to educate the public. You're a blessing to us all.

God bless and keep you strong.

S. C.

* * *

Dear Blanca,

I am a thirty-three-year old woman from Ohio with SMA Syndrome. I just want to say thank you, for everything. I am appreciative for meeting all the ladies in this group with SMA Syndrome, but especially you. You know more than my gastroenterologist. You are a Godsend.

This afternoon I received an email from a woman who saw the SMA Awareness posts on my blog advocating your Support Group. She went on to tell me that her daughter is in a similar situation as you and had to postpone her first semester of college due to illness. The doctors have (mis)diagnosed her with IBS and then an eating disorder yet she is not getting any better and she spoke of them losing hope. I suggested your group to her and sent her the links to all the research you have been kind enough to share with all of us. How amazing would it be, if your posts and the info you share with us all in the support group actually help direct her to a diagnosis that could save her life! That is true divine intervention.

Your Friend,

K Z.

* * *

Dear Blanca,

I am a fifteen-year-old from MO with SMA Syndrome. I was on a feeding tube for 9 months and a PICC line for 6 months. The doctors are scared to do surgery so now I am on an NJ tube. I have had the worst treatment plan ever! They made me see a psychologist, thinking I had anorexia.

I spent the entire first semester of my sophomore year in the hospital and went into liver failure on Christmas. Its now my first year back in school since my liver transplant and it is hard because people look at you differently. I went from being the happy cheerleader to now being the extremely sick kid who is never at school because of doctor appointments and hospital stays. I could only imagine how it would be in college, as you have experienced. My stomach still hurts all day, everyday and the only thing that helps is knee-to-chest position, sleeping on left side curled in a ball, and the heating pad. My teeth hurt sometimes and now I'm having lots of problems with blood counts and hormone balances... it seems like it never ends. Something always goes wrong :(

But it's been good to have the Lord and some of the best people in the world like you to have my back. Thank you for all the incredibly wonderful information you have shared with me! You are really like my guardian angel!!!! :) You have no idea how happy your work has made me. I would love to say that just made my day but I would just be lying. IT MAKES MY WHOLE LIFE! YOU ARE LIKE MY NEW HERO! It sounds like you have worked like crazy to deal with SMA Syndrome and make as "normal" of a life for yourself as possible. Keep your chin up! WE'RE IN THIS BOAT TOGETHER!

I firmly believe the good LORD brought you to me to help guide me and to make each other stronger and better fighters! :) Let's keep in touch.

Love,

K. D.

AFTERWARD

*(Essay Originally Published in 'Wide Awake'
Literary Magazine in 2010, Reprinted With
Permission)*

"The Angle of Agony":
Perspectives on Perpetual Physical
Pain from Longterm Illness

As the stabbing sensation grew sharper, I put
my chest to my knees, my hair flying into my
face. I slid from my seat and onto the cold,
tiled floor and began to cry, open-mouthed. A
few seconds later, my cries turned to screams.

I heard the doctor grab his phone from
his desk and push a few buttons. "Five milligrams of IV fentanyl, stat," he commanded.

In seconds, the door of his office banged
open and a black-haired nurse in pink scrubs
ran in with a syringe, roll of tape, cotton ball
and alcohol wipe. While she prepped a vein
on my right arm, the doctor pulled on a pair
of purple rubber gloves and took the syringe

in his hands. By this point, the pain was so consuming, I barely noticed as the needle entered my skin. It was no more than a single drum-beat in my massive, blaring symphony of agony.

Only moments later, I forgot.

I firmly believe that the moment pain dissipates, the human mind immediately begins to forget just how intense it truly was or what exactly it felt like—until it returns. I have gone through long periods in my life in which I continually felt some degree of physical pain, every minute of every day, and there were moments in which it all flared up beyond tolerable levels. These episodes are both unforgettable but completely forgettable. That is to say, every time it happened, I learned all over again just how terrible pain could be. I thought, 'there's no way it was this bad last time,' and would be fully convinced that only now was I experiencing the worst pain of my life.

Some facets of such an experience, however, cannot be forgotten. Longterm physical pain changes a person. Some changes are temporary, while others can last long after the pain dissipates—months, years, or even a lifetime. This essay explores the mind of the ill and how perpetual physical pain alters their perspectives and psyches as a whole.

First, I ask you to think back to your worst bout of illness. That week in bed, sipping tea and soup, home from work or school. It may be a bad cold, the flu, a sinus infection, gastroenteritis, pneumonia. Now, imagine the peak of that pain. Concentrate on the sheer intensity, and how it temporarily transformed your thoughts. Think of the hopelessness. The worry. The inability to form coherent ideas. The desperation to just make it stop, make it stop.

Now, imagine that pain lasting far more than a moment. More than a week. Or a month. Or a year. Or two. Imagine it filling every moment of every day, indefinitely, with no end in sight. Imagine it permeating every season, every holiday. Your birthday. Christmas. The first snowfall of the year. Movie night with the guys or girls. The weekly church service. It's there when you wake up, when you (try to) go to sleep. It's there when you shower. When you brush your teeth. When you open a book. When you put on a sock. When you try to pray.

In the short-term, pain makes one irritable, even those who naturally have the sweetest disposition. It shrinks the temper, magnifies minute annoyances in one's life, inclines one to want to make mountains out of molehills. This is why, during times of pain, one can learn who their true friends are—who sticks around in understanding and who is a "summer soldier" or "sunshine patriot." Who is around simply to take, and who understands that friendships are an alternating pattern of taking and giving, depending on the season of life.

It is well known that pain can be both a cause and consequence of stress. But, pain also reduces one's ability to handle unrelated stressful situations—like that exam coming up at school or that confrontation you had yesterday morning with your boss at work— both emotionally and physically. Physically, stress raises blood pressure, heart rate, and the production of potentially-harmful hormones like cortisol, to name just a few of the innumerable grueling side-effects. These effects are clinically shown to be magnified in those who are already under the significant stress of continual physical pain.

Pain can make even the most scholarly writers and experienced public-speakers horribly inarticulate. Even when not in crescendo, pain can place a haze on the mind. This "brain fog" can last long after a flare-up—as long as the pain is still at least humming in the background. The longterm-ill often feel as though they have lost the "spark" or "edge" of their intelligence, and this can lead to further despair and stress. I, who received a near-perfect score on the SATs and graduated college with a 4.0 grade-point-average, was unable to correctly spell the word "world" backward when asked at a doctor appointment.

The longterm-ill are prone to forgetting their "flame," as well. They become too tired, burned-out, and/or consumed by their pain to ponder the ambitions that once gripped their hearts with ferocity. They could grow weary upon simply hearing their friends discuss their vacation plans—involving travel, exploration, learning a language, or even the lesser-flashy activities like setting up an entertainment system in their basement, planting vegetables in their backyard, or cleaning out their attics so they can enjoy a new space.

Those in pain often have no ambition or passion beyond simply getting better. Days are no longer measured by the tasks accomplished or the number of new things learned, but simply, how bad the pain is. Those in constant pain are prone to stop planning or even thinking about the future altogether. Their perspectives can seem "selfish" to outsiders, as their outlook often goes no further than their "noses"—wondering, "how do I feel right now, and how can I make the pain go away or at least diminish enough so I can stand to live through the next minute?" Rather than learning that foreign language or exploring that exotic continent, their goal simply is whittled down to mere survival.

Pain can make one become like a child—helpless and carnal. Children are carnal in that when they experience hardship, they do not search for meaning, purpose or significance. They do not think, "what am I learning from this situation?" They do not seek the "beauty in the meltdown," at least not until they are older. And, as children are simply interested in immediate entertainment or pleasure, the perpetual-pain-patient just wants to feel okay right now. They do not have hindsight or vision. The search for significance often does not begin until far later, if/when the pain dips below a certain threshold.

The ill want others to take their pain seriously and know not to ask too much of them, but at the same time, they paradoxically do not want to be excluded, exiled, or treated too differently. Even when surrounded by encouraging friends, the most common emotion that patients in pain feel from day-to-day is isolation. They feel trapped by their bodies, as though in a cage. They feel as though they are watching their lives unfold from the outside looking in, or from a badly-tuned television set. They feel as though the world is passing them by and leaving them behind. Their bodies are always keen to put them "back in their place" whenever normal activity is attempted, and each such failure hurts as terribly as the last. However, they still want to be tempted by these activities. That is to say, they still want to be invited to all the same social events and trips as before. It feels good—validating, even—just to see their names on the invitation. It allows them to pretend that others believe they are still normal. It allows them to pretend that they actually are normal.

It allows them to have the power of an option to place a "no" RSVP, rather than having that decision pre-made for them by their friends, parents or doctors. It allows them to decide to come to that crazy sporting event anyway, if only just to bring the snacks and cheer their friends on from the sidelines.

Those in constant pain want sympathy, not pity. But, they never expect their friends to truly "know how they feel" and they certainly do not want to hear that line spoken to them when it is not true. It cheapens their suffering. One cannot possibly know how another feels unless they become that person. But, patients in pain want their friends to simply try to identify and sympathize—to patiently listen and learn—all the while under the mutual understanding that they will ultimately fail. The mere effort is enough, if it is a sincere one.

Often, less sympathy is offered to those who are sick but don't "look sick." Friends can be misled upon logging onto social networking sites and seeing photos of your smiling face. Those who are in your company just once or twice a week—at Sunday church service and Tuesday-night bible study, for example—may watch you behave somewhat "normally" for a handful of hours and come to the incorrect conclusion that you must be "fine" around the clock and your pain is not all that bad. They are unaware that, for every hour you pass in their presence looking "okay," you may spend ten hours at home alone, immobilized in agony. They do not know what a sacrifice of limited, daily "energy points" it was for you to go to that two-hour church service or that evening-long birthday party. They do not understand how difficult it was for you to act normally, concealing your pain behind a smile. Simple feats that the healthy take for granted—like sitting still in a pew for two hours—may require enormous amounts of effort on your part.

The longterm-ill often create two personas in their mind: the "old me" and "new me." Healthy me and sick me. Their lives are forever divided into the categories of "before" and "after" the pain began. Long-term pain can change one's outlook on life entirely, even after recovery is made. A recovered individual can oscillate—sometimes multiple times in the same day—between a frenzy of wanting to seize everything possible out of life to make up for time lost, and tiptoeing the line of normalcy with the uneasiness of a foreigner in a strange land. When immersed in the latter scenario, the recovered feel a terrible lack of confidence—a hesitance to trust their bodies ever again. Recovered individuals are often accustomed to their former inabilities and may feel simultaneous prickles of fear, anxiety, excitement and eagerness when returning to "normal" physical activity, like going to school or work, or taking a swim or stroll. They do not know their limits and often have a hard time relearning where they are. On some days, they celebrate their newfound freedom and push themselves to unhealthy extremes, perhaps even causing injuries or setbacks, while on other days they are inclined to budget their "energy points" tightly no matter how well they are feeling, as though still allotted only a tiny handful per day by their former illnesses. Wizened (or scarred) by their pasts, recovered patients often are still less likely to plan for the future, knowing how ethereal human abilities really are. They are less optimistic than they used to be, less naïve than their healthy counterparts who have never experienced similar physical trauma. They know firsthand how easily health can fail and earthly plans can fall through. They truly understand the extent of their own mortality.

All of this begs the question: Is there no hope? Is the purpose of this essay to demoralize? Am I writing this simply to emphasize the obvious fact that pain is bad? As a survivor of Superior Mesenteric Artery (SMA) Syndrome—an agonizingly painful, life-threatening, rare disorder that stole the "normalcy" from years of my youth—I am able to stand up and say with confidence that the answer to each of the above questions is "no." It is the strength of the Lord Jesus Christ that allows me to give that answer. The more time passes, the more I see the fingerprints of God's Glorious Hand on my own story and struggles. My blurry, short-sighted human eyes may have been far too weak to perceive all of this when my illness first began, but now I know for sure that everything happened for a reason—to bring me closer to Him (as storms often do), to teach me to lean not on my own human strength and understanding but His, to equip me to serve as a source of information and support to other rare disease patients and their families, and to give me a radically different testimony to share in order to spread His word. Even during the height of my illness—when I thought I would die before reaching my second decade of life—I derived comfort from the fact that my Lord and Savior has a 'glorified body' waiting for me in New Jerusalem. I knew that my glorified body surely won't have a narrow mesenteric angle, or the need to vomit every bite or cry when my blouse brushes my tummy the wrong way. I knew my glorified body will have enough muscle mass to walk—no, to *run,* and to leap.

And, I know now that no matter what comes my way next, I am always shielded, armed, and ready. Not by my own strength—the Lord Almighty knows that ran out long ago. I am running on the strength of Jesus Christ—my Great Physician, my Healer.

Love,

Samantha Mina

Lean more about SMA Syndrome at:
www.SMASyndrome.org.